IN

THE

AGE

OF

LOVE

IN THE AGE OF LOVE

Michael Stein

THE PERMANENT PRESS
Sag Harbor, New York 11963

Library of Congress Cataloging-in-Publication Data

Stein, Michael D.
    In the age of love / by Michael Stein.
        p. cm.
    ISBN 13: 978-1-57962-150-6 (hardcover: alk. paper)
    ISBN 10: 1-57962-150-3 (hardcover: alk. paper)
    1. Teachers—Fiction. 2. New Orleans (La.)—Fiction. I. Title.

PS3569.T3726I58 2007
813'.54—dc22   2006035861

The Permanent Press
4170 Noyac Road
Sag Harbor, NY 11963

For Justin and Anne

ALSO BY MICHAEL STEIN

<u>FICTION</u>

Probabilities
The White Life
The Lynching Tree
This Room Is Yours

<u>NON-FICTION</u>

The Lonely Patient

"Love is also memory."

—Eaven Boland

PART 1: ARRIVAL

JONATHAN

Leaving the two-room cabin on the lake in Burlington, Vermont unlocked, Jonathan Parrish climbed into his pickup and headed south toward the National Education Association conference in New Orleans. He gave himself two days to get there, two days for the meeting, and then a leisurely drive home if that's how it turned out. When he was on the job, he was willing to fly, but otherwise he was in no hurry. It was before seven in the morning, but he was not a good sleeper, and hadn't been since he turned forty a few years back. He was usually awake early enough to see the street lights go off on the roads on the other side of the lake, and that made for a lifetime of long days.

He stopped for coffee in town at the Waiting Room where he quietly read his *Sentinel* among the teenagers of Vermont who worked or played all night, the guitarists and furniture makers and skiers, the girls in overalls with fraying tapestry handbags and long gray scarves who lived up here near Canada in the wet and cold cobalt beauty and drove into town to open these stores. At 8:30, when the university officially opened, he walked to the pay phone in the back of the restaurant and called to remind his office he'd be away, and to leave them the hotel name and number. He thought of himself as a teacher of young children who happened, for the past few years, to work part-time on a college campus. He'd made his real living for the past decade when

UNICEF hired him to give advice to schools, cities, and countries, but he was really just a teacher. He went around the world because that's where the wars were, and when a war ended and there was no electricity or heat or running water, when buildings had no roofs or doors, when half the trained teachers were dead, he had some ideas as to how to help the children learn. Today, he was driving across his own continent to give a speech.

He hadn't taken out a cigarette with his coffee. He still had the self-control to reserve his cigarettes for driving time when he was away from people, and he didn't want some twenty-year-old letting him have it for polluting. After six years quit—the dollars saved went toward work on his father's house—he'd started smoking again seventy-two hours earlier when he finally understood that Lily Mayeux might not even agree to meet with him in New Orleans. Smoking wouldn't help his hockey. He was already one of the older players in the league and he could hear his teammates chiding him, "A defenseman who can't breathe. That's just what this squad needs for the play-offs." Climbing into the truck, he pulled open the ashtray and rested his coffee cup in it. But he knew, really, that the open tray meant he was preparing for later; he'd light up in a few hours when he crossed the White River.

He carried in his black leather shoulder bag a few clothes, a paper he was working on for the *American Journal of Education Studies*, and the latest red volume of a day book he'd kept nearly continuously for two decades. He threw the bag behind the front seat, on top of a cooler containing four Bosc pears, some Goya mango juice, and Swedish fish, his favorite candy. The sweet essentials. He was looking forward to this trip, the long hours alone when he could listen to the radio and think in peace. He was flexible in his musical tastes (Lily had given him that) and was willing to hear whatever the FM stations threw at him. He waited for the old Ford to heat up—this was one thing he shared with the youth of Vermont, a taste for decrepit but honorable cars—and thought this morning was the kind of frigid when he could have used the scarf Lily had once promised him. He was looking forward to New Orleans, but he had a mental checklist when he went off on assignments that he couldn't help going through this morning, although this was a pleasure trip mostly. That was too strong: it was a trip that had none of the pressure of his day-to-day job. It was like one of his work trips only in this way: he would arrive not knowing the cause or the ending.

He wore faded black jeans, a gray T-shirt under his favorite green V-neck sweater, and a tight gray, wool cap that made him look like any college kid on Church Street. When he had finished his coffee, a few miles past Montpelier, he spread on some lip balm, dipping his finger into a tiny blue tin. His lips had gotten burned during an unexpectedly sunny April afternoon of snow-shoeing the week before. Route 89 South was a winding road through the mountains. It was a lovely trip for an interstate, trailing along an old train line for a while and then running high over a river. He slowed often to study the towns of Vermont set below him in valleys—a few smokestacks, white or brick steeples of the churches, the distinctive green roofs. He was constantly struck by Vermont's beauty—the colonial era houses, solid Federal-style buildings and banks with unadorned granite steps, covered nearly year-round with snow—and his impossible good fortune in getting a university position. But when he drove this route, he also had a sense of dislocation: this was not really where he lived. It was too pretty, too clean and piney. He was grateful that the university had given him a teaching job, but at times, he missed the dangers of city life, the marvelous and strange and sur-reptitious in Marrakesh and Addis Ababa and Lima. Of course, he had the sense of dislocation even when he lived in New York, the men sleeping on paper bags like he'd seen in every foreign capital he'd flown out to.

One reason he liked Burlington was because, at forty-three years old, he felt he was among the city's oldest residents. Of course this wasn't so, but in the places he hung around—The Waiting Room, the Nordic ski trails, the university bookstore, the food cooperative—he rarely saw anyone over twenty-five. It was as if some invisible selection process had taken place, an epidemic had struck everyone with graying hair and he had been one of the lucky few survivors. He enjoyed the youth all around him, but encounters with women his age rarely took place.

While he smoked and crossed into New Hampshire and then Massachusetts, listening to Marvin Gaye and Al Green, he thought about the two relationships with women he'd had in the twelve years since Lily. Each of them had been long and serious, and he must have been in love both times, but never enough to marry, and without that lovers always eventually drifted apart, didn't they? He started thinking about Miriam just outside Philadelphia when the hard rock came on, and she was with him until Virginia, when country music filled the tuner. An actress, slight, beautiful, who never quite got enough work and lived with a small, but real desperation he thought of as passion for the longest time. In the last of their nearly five years together, Miriam had bought for the kitchen this small glass herbarium, a miniature greenhouse the size of a birdcage. In it, she had planted ivy and another vine, a kind of honeysuckle, and within months, it seemed to him, the two plants were too close inside, without enough room, struggling to get out, choking each other for sunlight.

His mind picked up Audrey outside of Virginia, as he headed into the Smokies and bluegrass stations. He'd been with her through most of the years in Atlanta, after he'd left New York. She was a researcher in the Vaccine Preventable Illness Division at the Centers for Disease Control, with a gift for mathematics. She claimed that she never wanted to marry or have children. He knew her clenched jaw by heart. It was there when he didn't ask a question in the right way or failed to respond correctly. Was there ever the right thing to say to her? His level of concern wasn't high enough; he wasn't adequately supportive; was he trying to be mean or funny? She couldn't tell, and by the end, neither could he. He didn't understand women; the women he had been with had informed him of this handicap, and he'd grown accustomed to feeling ignorant, and not trusting his own tone, his answers. When he called her three years after they split and he'd left Georgia for San Francisco, Audrey told him she was the mother of two, and that her husband was a pilot for Delta.

His work life was so different from his private life. As a teacher, Jonathan Parrish wanted to understand what happened to a child in war. He believed everything was knowable. Take a few clues, pry a little, regard what you learned seriously and with sophistication and it all became clear. But privately he was able to acknowledge mystery. He trusted the oddness of coincidence, of chance meetings. He thought dreams had meanings even if they weren't immediately evident. Not all could be revealed. Everything about another's life was not knowable. His work with the adults in other countries who, in the midst of their own losses taught young students, was about organization and making do, and was beyond emotion. He had an appetite for the long hours and a suitability; his work was never wearing. At home, he had less nerve, and a cowardly inability to admit when things were going badly, or maybe his pain threshold was high, or perhaps he was shy in delivering bad news to himself.

As the oldest brother of three, he'd taken on a parental role at a young age, and always heard the bad news first, experience which served him well in war zones. Over the years, his brothers called if they really needed something, a loan or the name of a doctor; he was the only one who'd finished college, who had some money in the bank for an emergency. When his brother Paul's youngest broke his pelvis and femur in a car accident, he'd flown directly to Newport News to scout the surgeons and to take care of Paul's two older boys who needed driving to games and lessons. That week in his brother's place reminded him of the days in their parents' house. As a boy in a small town in northwest Connecticut, an only child for quite a few years (his parents next had Paul eight years later), he had kept to himself. He rode his bicycle to the great stone library in town (maybe that's why he liked Vermont), where he read poems and looked at botany books. His brothers were still in middle and elementary school, wearing his hand-me-downs, when he was paying for college himself. There, he worked in the main kitchen and learned Spanish from the dishwashers, the older men (he thought of them as old although, thinking back, they were probably in their 30's) who sat with him outside under the hot air vents during their breaks and laughed at his gringo mistakes; this language training stood him well during his work in Nicaragua.

He knew that because so many of their calls were associated with requests, his brothers felt bad bothering him when there wasn't a crisis. They didn't understand that a good news phone call wouldn't have been an interruption; he wasn't *that* busy. Especially since moving to Vermont a few years back. They would have interrupted him building a stone wall, or planting his tomatoes, or rowing on Lake Champlain, or what else, drafting a new report? But because they so often expected advice when they called, he'd grown into the habit of giving it to them, and they were probably right not to phone if they didn't want to hear what he thought of their latest job offer, or the prom night trouble of a daughter.

He rarely attended education professionals' meetings, preferring to stay away from crowds and large hotels. But his interviews from southern Africa six months before had caused a stir in all the national papers and he had been invited to give the featured talk at this Fiftieth Anniversary convention of 1984, an honor he couldn't refuse. His inviters sent the standard letter asking him to send along any audiovisual requests, offering the history of former featured speakers and the temperature of New Orleans in April, as well as a list of this year's attendees. As Jonathan flipped through the thirty pages of names and addresses (he had always been amused that teachers wanted so badly to know the company they kept), he saw Lily's.

When he read her name it was as if an era had suddenly come to an end. A peaceful decade dating back to 1973 when he met Miriam and was able finally to think of Lily as a woman he'd truly loved and, after considerable sadness, gotten over. She had presumably moved on, and he had too, becoming busy and successful beyond any expectation, and found his footing and his passion. He'd heard that she had become a teacher, but he hadn't known where she lived, what grade or grades she taught, or anything else about her life.

Seeing her name opened some secret chamber of his heart and he closed it quickly that day six months ago. Still, he taped her address next to the typewriter on his desk and did nothing. He thought of her often, and each time it reminded him of being awakened by the weight of a large cat, his long-haired Clementine: he'd want to push her off, but he'd want her to come back a little later for another visit.

He drove fast but calmly through the Smokies. Already it had been a drive of a thousand speculations about Lily, about his wrong decisions and regrets, and he was in a restless state, smoking steadily now. The further south he drove, the more life had closed in upon memories that perhaps rightly belonged in the past. Yet the visit with Lily Mayeux he had been visualizing for months suddenly seemed bewilderingly unlikely. If he decided to call her room when he finally arrived at his New Orleans hotel, his voice would just as likely engender a resistance, a bitterness, as it would a positive response. It would make sense if Lily would have nothing more to do with him; having him close by was probably the last thing she wanted. When it had ended so abruptly with her, *he* was responsible; *he* had made a mistake he now understood with twelve years of hindsight; he had never felt grievously wronged by her. Still, as he smoked and drove, he had the feeling he used to have around her, a feeling from back when they knew one another well, a combination of illicit thrill and stage fright, of pure hope. She had never been harmless. She had been dangerous to their neighborhood as a girl (wasn't she the one who accidentally set fire to the new book section of the town library with an unfinished cigarette?), and to him.

He kept his black bag packed. A habit after years of leaving town on a few hours' notice. It was a young person's game flying to other continents, but he still hadn't been able to give it up completely. The call came in and the rushed preparation began: rental cars, hotels, airline tickets, and clearance for each from someone different at the United Nations. Get cash. Load his shoulder bag with articles to read that might provide some context for the war zone he was about to enter. Talk to a few colleagues who had lived in the part of the world where he was headed. Fly out, preparing to talk to the press when he landed to explain who had invited him. Meet the local officials who called, and come up with a plan. Certainly, he'd have to do a survey of the teachers and some families (once he found them) to figure out what they thought of school before the war. Ten drafts of the survey so he didn't miss the key question. Work all night, interviewing more people. Sometimes he received lots of help. Once in the Philippines, the ministry of education had arranged for ten teachers and ten telephones in a high school gym to help make calls. Other times he was on his own. One phone call after another to strangers who were still grieving: tell me everything about your children. No one *had* to talk to him about their history, but they did. He was Jonathan Parrish, from the United Nations, in town to help. Late at night, after his last cold call, he'd phone Miriam or Audrey, who each had asked him to give up the pace and frequency of his time away.

He had never married, so the women he met around Burlington asked him questions about his "earlier" life because it was continuous with the one he was living, because he was unpredictable (which at forty-three was synonymous with having no wife and/or having severe emotional difficulties), because he didn't behave the way they expected. They assumed that he would be difficult to get to know, so they asked him questions innocently. Why Vermont? Was this really the first house he'd ever owned? Did he really mean it when he said he was trying to stay put, make a home? Because he was unmarried, they sometimes saw him as the embodiment of suffering, at other times as the likely cause of past suffering. When the time inevitably came that they asked him to confirm a history of romantic disappointment, he didn't. Again unexpected. They felt duped, let down, because they wanted to love him for his unacceptable heartbreaks, for his losses of Miriam, of Audrey. Of course he never told any of them Paul's half-humorous, half-serious long-time explanation for his bachelorhood—that he was waiting for Lily Mayeux. Not someone *like* Lily, but Lily herself.

He kept in his closet an olive green cap Lily had knit for his birthday in 1972. He had been surprised that she had such a skill, that an intelligent woman like Lily, who had the money to buy whatever she wanted, would take the time to knit. He had always been impressed by her patience. He shouldn't have been surprised that she'd also ended up a teacher, putting in the long hours of coursework and testing. He remembered that she wouldn't show him the cap while she was working on it. He remembered that from week to week she would measure him—ear to ear, a tape around his forehead. He remembered she'd promised him a matching scarf. He hadn't worn the cap in years. Before he threw it in his leather bag this morning behind the front seat, he checked to see if it had been eaten by moths.

As he crossed Alabama, it was not hard for him to remember what Lily was like at twenty-three, even how she looked back then. She'd given him a playful picture of herself wrapped around the roots of a gigantic copper beech tree that had been pulled up by a backhoe in their neighborhood. She wore a brown sweater and her thin arms and legs followed the root system so that she was nearly invisible against the clods and stones, her red hair hanging amidst the web of sticks. That was what she was like: ready to clown around and get dirty. He remembered being attracted to her when she came by the house in Connecticut a few days before heading back to college for her junior year, but not being able to name the physical ache in his upper chest until the first time she visited him in New York.

He didn't want to see her in New Orleans. It was risky to stir up what he'd left behind; any meeting with her would be strained and awkward. He had wished the best for Lily, and seeing her would not make anything better.

LILY

On the plane, when she finally had the time to reopen the envelope containing the conference materials, she had been thinking to herself: it will be a pleasure to be away from home, to have three days to myself in New Orleans. At home these days, her husband paid more attention to his troubles at work than to her. Of course, she was the same way, and, in addition, favoring little Ben with her time; she was a mother first, a wife second. Wasn't that true for every woman with small children, even for the mothers of her older students? Of *course:* children gave what a spouse couldn't, the shaping of time by need. She loved her husband; Peter was a good man, and they were a good team. But these days conversations were about pick-ups and drop-offs and dinners and bedtimes, the details of parental collaboration, and rarely about her work or his, or the world in general outside their house.

She didn't realize her work mattered so much until times like these, when she was alone on a plane headed to New Orleans to the first conference she'd been to in years. It wasn't that she didn't want to think about her family; it was that she didn't want to think *only* about them. She worked from 8 to 3 every day and picked up her boy at day care on the way home; her husband would meet Ben at Greenmeadow when she was away and she worried about the change in routine for both of them. But she secretly enjoyed packing as she prepared for this trip. She liked the idea that she could fit everything she really needed in life (except Ben of course) in a single bag, that her life could be simplified like that. A few pieces of underwear, the latest volume of her black diary, sneakers, make-up (in case she needed a disguise), a toothbrush, her knitting. The rest of what she owned was superfluous and could easily be walked away from.

The night before she had been amazed to see Jonathan Parrish's name under FEATURED PRESENTERS in the program. She was strangely transfixed by his name in print. It seemed a miraculous coincidence when she first saw it as she was packing her clothes, the conference materials spread across her bed. She'd certainly thought of it over the years, but had had no occasion to see the two words, Jonathan Parrish, in typeface. She was immediately unsettled by the idea of seeing him. Today, his name took possession of her so that she felt swollen and melancholic as she rose from her aisle seat to ask the flight attendant for another club soda. She was not prepared to think of Jonathan nearby, or that she might run into him.

During their first years apart, when she wasn't angry at the very thought of him, she had sometimes wondered what might have happened if she'd waited for Jonathan Parrish. Back then, it seemed as if she was always waiting for his return from one of his Third World journeys with no clear timetable and no easy way to reach him in an emergency. What if she had followed him to Nicaragua in 1972? As what? His skill-less girlfriend? At twenty-three she had been convinced it was impossible to imagine a future with Jonathan, being left alone for months while he was gone. No matter how completely she loved him, no matter how well he treated her when they were alone, sealed into a room for a weekend when she couldn't get enough of his talk and touch. She wasn't that patient.

She had dated Peter Gorsky during sophomore year and she started up with him again after Jonathan. Peter was working in his family business just outside Boston, a few hours away from Windsor, and being with him reassured her that she had the right instincts. She was relieved to be with Peter. He spent long hours at work, but he didn't disappear into the jungle for months.

She knew exactly how her life would happen with Peter, step by step, safe and secure.

Peter had teased her that morning about her fear of flying. On the way to the airport the wind was loud in the car, the tree limbs bouncing, even the birds unsure of themselves in the heavy gusts that snapped the flags outside the terminal.

It was a rough flight, the refreshment carts stowed prematurely due to turbulence. It was hard not to think of her sister Cynthia who longed for these bumpy rides. Boarding a plane, Cynthia was excited by a breeze blowing in, a darkening sky, by thunder. She had been a great risk taker, thirsty for strong feeling, for scuba and rock-climbing, for howling dogs and howling men who were always looking for her to make them happy. Peter had never met Cynthia; Lily rarely spoke about her with him.

She took up her knitting. The act of knitting did for her what smoking did for smokers. It was a way to fidget without thinking, but it had the advantage over smoking of social desirability. Outside, water beaded on the tiny window and she could see the ground beneath them now, the brown Mississippi River. As she knit, she liked touching the yarn and feeling it go through her fingers, a hyphen-worth at a time, more or less—it was amazing how quickly a hundred yards got used up, when each stitch was so small. There was also a nice ongoing meditation, sometimes quite conscious and other times not at all, on the person for whom she was making the garment.

In those first years, she had enforced some private rule about not contacting Jonathan Parrish. Keep Jonathan at a distance, and thereby keep him abstract. She never told herself that she was better off without him, but she convinced herself that he would never have changed his relentless work schedule, his mind always traveling somewhere. She felt badly when she thought of him, the pain they had caused each other; that made it easier to stay away. If she had called over the years, he might have thought she was trying to put something over on him, that she was pretending she wanted something that she didn't really want. With the distance of twelve years, her picture of Jonathan Parrish was of a man who was captivating and bright, and a little sad. She thought about how memory was like the healing of skin: at first the scar is definite and later becomes blurred.

PART 2: FRIDAY AFTERNOON

LILY

She walked around the hotel room hoping he hadn't read through the attendee list; even if he saw her name—unlike his, which was prominent as a Presenter, hers was listed among the hundreds of "Participants"—there was no reason to believe he would seek her out.

At a conference of this size, over six thousand in attendance, chances were they wouldn't meet. More than likely he would pretend not to recognize her if they passed each other in the hotel corridor. He would have his own misgivings. His anger with her could have easily lasted twelve years; she expected it had.

She thought of calling home to report she had landed safely. Peter would work on some house project in her absence. He was a wonderful carpenter. He had recently built a tree house for Ben, complete with screen windows and a skylight.

She liked the old house in Maine best of all the houses they'd lived in over the years: the bathroom door that didn't quite close; the dark stain in front of the refrigerator where some previous tenant had allowed water damage to leave its mark. Peter wanted each defect corrected, but she actually treasured the holes and warpings and faults.

The red light on her phone had been blinking since she stepped into her room.

When I learned that you had taken a teaching position in Maine, I was delighted you'd landed in such an interesting and hospitable place. I hope our paths cross this weekend.

She was astonished to find his voice in her ear. She listened to his thirty words twice, wanting to delete them—have him go away for another twelve years—but during her third replay, she thought too of the many reasons that she would be interested to see him again: because it would be brave to see him, because such a meeting would be evidence that she refused to take any prescribed view of herself or of Jonathan Parrish.

Like a body's scent that doesn't change, she knew his code. Leave it open, leave it up to her. She was annoyed that the burden of choice was again hers. She sensed their paths would cross soon whether or not she answered him; he'd found her in New Orleans after all. What did he want? She knew, whatever the motives which she wasn't ready to examine just then, she would have a lot to think about if she *didn't* face him, sit across from him in a matter-of-fact way, for a voluntary, controlled, poignant hour, and this irritated her and made her feel trapped. If she actively tried to avoid him, she would feel silly and juvenile and it would ruin these few days away. She would probably look back on this trip as a wasted opportunity; she was curious to know what had happened to Jonathan Parrish. After twelve years, there was nothing to worry about: they would be drastically unalike by now, she thought. One hour with Jonathan and done; maybe she'd even enjoy it. There was no telling. His tone sounded kind, genuinely pleased. If they did meet, she would wear a sweater, even in the heat: something modest but pretty, that would allow her to feel covered up.

After this resolution, the decision to respond to his message came so swiftly it made her nervous and she practiced the words she would leave on his phone machine twice, before, in a moment of enthusiasm free of paranoid restraint, she replied, *If you have time for lunch, it would be good to see you. I will be the 5' 8" woman sitting in the hotel restaurant at noon on Friday.*

She was sitting in a corner booth, drinking iced tea, watching the overhead fan that was turning fast one way, but which presented a pattern that turned slowly the other way. Just a trick of the visual system (a topic she taught in ninth-grade biology) and the width and speed of the fan blades, she thought. Every so often, she casually looked toward the door.

When he came in, he looked a little disheveled, as if he'd been up all night. His wide green eyes looked directly at her. He was wearing a tight black sweater jacket, like a young skier might, as if he'd arrived from another season. It made him look even slimmer than she remembered, the muscles of his chest fuller. His shoulders were always a little heavier than his clothes suggested. The moss green eyes, the voice, (were those gray hairs?), the easy way he moved all disturbed her. She looked away, down at the floor; his clogs were black leather and beaten. He still wore clogs.

She was facing the door and he walked unhurriedly toward her table.

"I'm sorry to bother you but I'm looking for. . . ," he said, the hint of a playful smile played on his dry lips.

"She's here."

"I didn't know if she would be when I arrived."

"Where else would she be? But you found your way, didn't you?"

Seeing him, her first thought was: why did he call me, to make trouble? She'd only grown more bothered since hearing his voice on her hotel phone. But she has told herself that if she heard anger in her voice during this lunch hour, she would try to disguise it. Better to keep it light. Jonathan always told her that she was a good kidder; she used to tease him and make him laugh. She would do that today. Oddly, this conversational strategy of light humor was the opposite of what she'd planned when she'd invited him, when she had thought to be careful and slow with

Jonathan. In either case, she would remain hidden. She would fill the air with words she knew by heart—the reports she'd give her aunt Sally during the annual call, stories about her sister, her job.

Jonathan had always been provocative and challenging. She remembered that from before; he had probed too much, or at least that's what she told herself then. He asked so many questions of her. She came to expect his interrogations. When she asked whether he thought a class she was taking assigned too much work, he asked ten questions—what other teachers expected, what were the actual readings—before he offered an opinion, an opinion which was not always reassuring. His inquisitiveness was not directed only at her. It was his way of moving through the world; he was interested in so many things. He was fascinated by people, and they naturally told him their stories. She had seen it: waitresses in restaurants, the super in his building in New York, even the mailman. He was curious and this scared her the year she turned twenty-three. She feared he would find something not to like if he got to know her entirely well, and that she would learn something about herself that she didn't want to know.

His constant probing: that was the best she could come up with when trying to understand her discomfort with this meeting. She'd had lunch alone with men before, but they were essentially strangers, other teachers at her school. With Jonathan she couldn't forget the things she knew. And neither would he. No talk at lunch could fix the difficult past. She had been hesitant to meet him because she expected censure from Jonathan Parrish. That is, if she didn't keep the conversation modest and easy.

She had decided, before answering his message, that *she* was curious about *him*. When she saw his full and clear face, the faint lines around his eyes, she allowed herself to relax. After all, she had invited him to lunch when she didn't have to.

JONATHAN

He arrived at the restaurant on time and she was already waiting in a light sweater whose color, turquoise, he remembered her favoring. This was new; when they were together, he had always waited for her: her train to roll into Grand Central Station, her call at midnight to his apartment. Today she was waiting and he felt shy, ready to back off. Had this piece of her character changed? Did she run according to clock-time, setting her watch early now that she had classrooms of children to get in and out? Or was this simply maturity—the expected changes from someone he knew only as a young woman?

He was moved that there was a book Lily had brought to read while she waited, placed on the table next to her setting. He saw it was a book about nature: *Magnificent Trees*, he read upside down. She used to read to him in bed in New York, he remembered. The dinner dishes would still be out. Garlicky steam, fried onions, old grease would be haunting the summer air, and she would read to him in her thin white nightgown, the top buttons undone her body luminous, sweat in the hollow of her neck, laying on the cool sheets. The smell of the restaurant was mixed up with this image of Lily, and it had been all these years and she was near him again, and he was glad she had returned his call.

He remembered describing to Lily, when she first visited his apartment twelve years before, how he had taken on the parental role with his brothers after their mother, the reader in the family, died. They had been a happy contented family until death swooped down in its pointless way when he was fourteen. The day of the funeral, the house was full of adults moving in slow motion or sitting in folding chairs against the wall; his grandmother making phone calls and his sobbing aunts grabbing anyone who passed for hugs. Neighbors, people from around town, all said they were sorry about his mother's death, trying not to say it while he listened, speaking to his father.

In the following weeks, Jonathan often found his father asleep in the kitchen with the newspaper on his knees. He sometimes spoke about his wife, but he did not manage so well without her. For his father, each room of the house contained different memories of her—cleaning here, cooking there, eating her favorite peach ice cream. Jonathan liked to remember his mother laughing so hard (he was always her co-conspirator), the only noise was a little click somewhere in the back of her throat.

The Mayeux sisters, as neighbors, as babies, must have been in his house the day of the funeral. Years later, when Lily was probably eight or nine, he remembered waving at the three of them swinging their legs on a stone wall in front of their house. Lily was always sitting between the older Cynthia and the younger Clare. Always together, waving at him as he drove past, each year the three had been a regular feature of his return visits to Windsor, when he came to see his father after a posting in Nicaragua, Bangladesh, Mozambique.

Lily had been a little girl every time he passed that stone wall in Windsor, until the night she wasn't and she'd come over to the house for a visit. Then his heart leapt when she walked into the room and looked him in the eye and frowned at his battered shirt and clogs. He looked away. He was talking to one of his brothers about Nixon's election.

He was struck by her transformation into a sparkling twenty-two-year-old, great legs in black tights marked by musical notations, clefs and chords. As she unbuttoned her coat, he glanced at her fingers working the fabric and he couldn't look at her for another few minutes. His body felt something, and his eyes, in a form of protection, wouldn't let any more of her into his brain. He was feeling strangely nervous, vibrant.

He set out to make her smile. Her eyes were barely open, her lids crinkled and her lips thinned when she finally laughed, and he noticed she wore lipstick and thought, she's too young for lipstick. She's just a girl sitting on a stone wall. She was not flirting, but he wanted her to, and then she decided they should catch fireflies.

He liked to believe that Lily was his personal discovery, but really *she* had found *him* during that summer visit to Windsor when he was thirty. She invited him to chase fireflies in the woods near her house, six streets from his in Windsor. He had been visiting from New York where he was stationed with the United Nations. It had been a painfully clear night and the flies, before they blinked off then on again, were like the stars they could see at every clearing and field they crossed of the once-farmed acres. It was the first night that she was not merely the little girl down the block who grew up playing with his two younger brothers. She knew that he knew her reputation: as the youngest on the street she could do what she liked—outgrow all the boys, bite their fingers during fights, destroy them in swim races. She had been the indestructible one, the daddy's girl—Mr. Mayeux defended her misdeeds—and as a result had grown wild. She was the one who nearly burned down the library and had burned a few hearts as well.

He asked her what he was to do with the fireflies once he'd caught them. "Let them go," she said. It was that month they became lovers. He remembered feeling his future had arrived.

"You're a lucky man," his brothers told him when he called them after her first visit to New York three weeks later. They had always liked Lily, her effortless ease around people, her oversized jewelry, her long legs that had beaten them in sprints since they were boys.

During their year together, he was away as much as he was home. He would often return from his time abroad angry. Angry that there were places where there were no medicines, where there was no clean water, where malnourished babies died in mud-floored huts in hot air thick with flies. It galled him. In places where there were wars, simple, treatable ailments killed the poor even after the fighting ended; then there were the outbreaks of meningitis, tetanus, even measles murdering a family at a time. He felt like weeping. When he arrived in New York, he would be jarred by his apartment, its hot water and electricity, the light that came on in the refrigerator. At home, he felt inactive, that he was not doing enough with his life. He felt most alive helping people, kneeling in the red dirt of a sugar cane field. He liked underdogs, working for the sure losers. It cheered him when poor people didn't give up; it restored his faith.

Lily had made all the first moves. The day she first touched him; the morning she first kissed him; the afternoon she first undid his clothes. He was comfortable having her do these things, but she was a little embarrassed afterward about how fast they happened, how she had pursued him.

This time, *he* had called her. The lunch invitation was unexpected.

LILY

In the old days, his first gaze was always one of enormous intensity. Today, as he came toward her, she was judging the distance from the last time they saw one another. After the information had been gathered, there was a moment when she looked away before locking in again. She remembered he had always visibly desired her, although that wasn't in his eyes now.

She first spent an extended time with him after his surgery, twelve years before. Paul had called from New York, two days after Jonathan's appendectomy.

She had met them at the hospital: "Here I am and I want to help." Otherwise he would have been alone, she knew; Paul was flying home to his wife and new baby.

"Once you take care of a sick man, once you see him gaunt and needy, he will follow you anywhere, he'll never abandon you," her sister Clare had told her.

Jonathan leaned on her, walking the worn, chipped, and uneven marble steps up to his second floor apartment in Fort Washington Heights. The hallways of his building smelled of cigarettes and sour cream and olive oil and damp towels. Jonathan hadn't taken a vow of poverty, but he might as well have, he lived so frugally. His apartment had bookshelves consisting of planks on cinder blocks; there was no air conditioner, just a fan without its cover, the blades exposed; he could have used new sheets.

The first evening at home, Jonathan's temperature went up. His face glowed red and he trembled. She read to him from *Anna Karenina* (she loved the fat Russian novels she read over and over); the pace was slow enough that whole chapters could be skipped when he dozed off. Throughout the night he snapped awake and wanted to talk about his work. He was just starting to travel then into war zones, but he had already formed opinions. He believed you took care of the youngest and least educated first, rather than let them remain ignorant for a day longer, because they were the hardest to save. He believed knowledge was power, except with the poor. He believed you could halt the spread of sexually transmitted disease by giving all women jobs, but first they had to be taught to read. She could see him against the baked brown landscape and walls of verdant mountains where he traveled by donkey and jeep. The roads were impassible even in good weather, she'd learned; he'd told her he was more likely to die from a collision with a passing vehicle than from a short flight in one of the single engine puddle-jumpers he regularly rode in.

She didn't mind being woken every few hours. She called him delirious when he interrupted himself to say he liked the way she smelled.

Sweat soaked his T-shirt that first night, and at daybreak she ran a bath and helped him in. A bar of April sunlight slanted across his back. As he lay in the deep narrow tub's grainy water, she sat beside him, wiped his face and under his arms with a warm, damp washcloth, and adjusted the porcelain taps behind his head. The design of the bathroom floor, inlaid with tiny marble tiles, gave the room a medieval air.

His scar; she thought it would scare her. At first she wouldn't look into the water.

She had been scared in a different way the summer before, when she first went to meet him at this apartment. She thought that her fear emanated from New York itself where anything could happen, anything at all. But sometime during the early fall she understood it wasn't the city, it was him. He had a power over her that wasn't always comfortable. The urgency, the pressure she felt on the train into the city from Hartford, was the necessity of seeing him. She felt out of control when she approached the city, but hadn't yet seen him outside on the platform waiting for her; that's when New York seemed most dangerous. And it all went away in the ecstatic unreality of his apartment when they had nothing to do but devour each other and leave one another's skin raw. There was nothing she wouldn't do with him.

"Visiting with the sick is a waste of time, don't you think?" he asked, taking the washcloth from her, soaking it, and running it gently across *her* forehead, *her* lips, excess water dripping onto the front of her blouse. On the floor beside him, cool air slid from the windowsill across the tiles onto her bare feet. "It's always uncomfortable, isn't it, the conversations falsely delicate?"

Sometimes his blunt honesty was disconcerting and she wondered if it was meant to drive her away. Was he testing her? At times, he seemed to be *trying* to be difficult and rude so as to force her to reconsider whether she really loved him. But it was at that moment in the bath when she realized that under his moodiness lay hidden a need for affirmation. If a man took on more than he could fix in the world, he needed reassurance. She understood for the first time that Jonathan Parrish had freed himself from what might have been despair by seeking out the suffering of others. This seeming selflessness offered a kind of immunity, but it was an incomplete one.

"Spoken like a true pessimist," she answered. "You'd prefer to lie here all alone?"

"Actually, no. Why don't you join me?"

She undressed and climbed into the tight slippery space facing him, feet touching feet. She had never avoided his body, which close-up she took in as a collection of blurry circles and semi-circles: chest, shoulders, face. His first touch made her nipples hard. Whenever he touched her, she felt like she hadn't been touched in a million years.

His scar didn't scare her. She didn't so much want to look away as to stare at it, touch it, remember it. She studied the sutures, the sewed-up lips on the wall of his belly. Where she touched the incision under the water, he had no sensation. "That's normal. It takes time to come back."

Clare was correct. There was a freedom that came out of seeing someone through an illness from the side of their bed. The sick kept nothing to themselves and so, as their attendant, you didn't have to either, for illness was a candor beyond words, a state where you could be judged and shamed, and if you weren't, but rather simply cared for, an unexpected closeness resulted, founded on the enormous relief of passing through it with another as your witness.

The note he'd sent to Hartford that week thanked her. "Your first classroom, I enjoyed being your student."

Lunch would only last an hour and then she could put these memories away for good. She almost regretted having this particular one, it was too intimate, and made her sad.

JONATHAN

He expected a nearly ordinary lunch with Lily, nothing strange or awkward. It would be fine. He wanted a deep drag on a cigarette. He wanted its burn in his mouth, and he wanted to hold the smoke inside like a ghost. Studying Lily again, he let himself see the past.

She spent five days tending to him after his appendectomy. She had arrived from Hartford where she was living after college; she had just taken her graduate school entrance examinations, and was thinking of becoming a teacher. He had just begun to work for UNICEF and was away as much as he'd been home that winter. The surgery enforced a needed rest.

He was delighted to see her, and in the cab from the hospital two days post-op, trying to absorb her presence, he was tongue-tied.

"If I need to go out, don't do any housework," she teased, once he was settled knowing he could barely move. She was going out to buy candles and wine and fruit and new linens.

"I'll try not to."

"Good."

"I'm a little light-headed," he said.

"You mean giddy. That's from being with me."

He remembered her sitting beside his tub one morning, light showing evenly on the checkered tile floor, Lily wearing a sleeveless peach blouse. He remembered the smoothness and long oval beauty of her upper arms when she held up the book she was reading aloud. He'd been up most of the night, he recalled, talking to Lily for hours about his work and his travels. Awake, minutes seemed like hours; asleep, hours seemed like minutes. At twenty-three she was more interested in the children he reported on, rather than the schools he was trying to fix. Why did that child die of salmonella—what actually made them die? And she wanted to hear about the mothers of these children. Lily grew very serious during these stories; she would put aside her novel to listen. She would study him, her lips pursed in concentration.

What was she reading to him that night and morning? He remembered it was a long book, one of her favorites. He was delighted she might enter a teacher training program. Wasn't their time together part of the reason for her decision to do so?

After the bath, she lay down next to him. She quickly fell asleep. He had always been envious of her ability to sleep well. When she exhaled her lips vibrated a little. He was amazed by her beauty which she was probably unaware of. Someone was playing a bass in the apartment next door, the broken music quite lovely. He kept his eyes shut and tried not to think of anything. He could feel his fever breaking, and gradually he grew a little drowsy. When he was nearly asleep, her face came closer to his, and he couldn't tell if she was awake or not until she put her arms around him, until there was kissing, and pressing together.

A kind of serenity settled on him, a surprising peace of mind given the pain.

On the fifth day he was reluctant to let her leave.

He remembered the year with Lily as a series of images. Her elegant handwriting on expensive note paper, Moorish in its complexity, O's like pools, A's like archways hung with ivy. Her short red hair shining above her ear. Their mutual enjoyment of weather and the air changing, the evening outside his windows, when everything became obscured. Lily stepping into the tub, putting her hands on his shoulder, and his licking her breast while she lowered herself; the sight of her nakedness frightened him he wanted it so much. Their laughing at the same things: a dog's feet going out from under him when he chased a cat around a corner of yellow linoleum. Walking in the Cloisters at the northern tip of Manhattan, eyes closed, describing to each other whole landscapes by the sounds of the rain: Its patter on the path was different from its sound on the tulips and the iron fence and the stone fountains.

Her simplest gestures—the way she turned and waved—dazzled him.

But there was one gesture that had been unforgettable. She would be looking hard at him, then lightly touch her index finger to her lips and move it to his face, easy and flowing, usually touching just below his lower eyelid where the eyelash had fallen. Her touch, combined with her curiosity of what he wished for as he blew the lash from her drying fingertip, had a special significance. It was a gesture that belonged to Lily, one he associated only with her. It meant that she had studied him, found something of his that she could offer back to him, a lash that carried access to some yearning.

LILY

Out of the corner of her eye, someone in the restaurant waved at her, but she didn't bother to look over to see who it was. Her sadness had brought on another memory.

When Cynthia had died suddenly of a cerebral hemorrhage, her father was broken. With Clare living in London, Lily came home immediately from Hartford to be with him and her mother. The night she arrived in Windsor, she did what Jonathan had told her to do if there was an emergency: leave word at the American Express office in Managua.

Her father's hair had gone white overnight; his clothes became a little more careless; his poise faltered. Her father's old beauty had vanished with unexpected suddenness. When she asked one evening what she could do for him, her father answered, "Stop seeing that man." He said it as if it were Cynthia's dying wish.

During the first few days after the awful unexpectedness of Cynthia's death, it seemed an aberration that Jonathan hadn't responded immediately to her telegram, to the messages she'd left with the Nicaraguan embassy and the United Nations office in New York. Worried something had happened to him, she sent a second telegram to Nicaragua with trembling hands. But then he still hadn't called. Desperately, she tried to form an argument in her mind for his not calling; she had believed he would simply fly to Windsor and appear.

Weeks passed, and at the funeral, alone and angry and confused, she felt a coldness in her stomach. Why hadn't he called? Jonathan had never let her down before. She considered, then dismissed the possibility that he could have been transformed by his own history of grief into a man who couldn't comfort her in her worst moments. And this was the worst.

The night she arrived from England, Clare had asked sharply, "Where's Jonathan?"

"I don't know," Lily had answered. "Somewhere in Nicaragua. I can't reach him."

"You tried?"

"I sent two telegrams."

"He values the lives of people he doesn't know, but when it comes to you, he can't even take care of a basic obligation," Clare answered with more than a trace of disdain in her voice.

It was as if Clare had heard and assumed all her father's opinions of Jonathan: even if he had an excuse, what kind of person was unreachable? What could that mean for a future together? How reliable would Jonathan Parrish ever be if he simply disappeared for weeks? Clare was convinced that he was the type of man who could be anywhere at all, but who would never commit to a decision to stay in one place. Lily knew that whatever words he would have to explain himself weren't important; he had not responded to her need.

Clare's complaints about Jonathan only reminded her of how much she missed him. She'd called his brothers, who told her Jonathan was in the jungle, but if he'd received her messages he would be trying to reach her. She missed Cynthia, who would have reassured her about Jonathan and calmed Clare and their father, who had never spoken of Jonathan again after his four-word command: Stop seeing that man. Her mother, sad and confused and not knowing what to say, could not soften Clare's tone. Clare attacked every defense of Jonathan as too little, too feeble, too unconvincing; her case against Jonathan only grew stronger as the days passed until Lily made up her mind that she didn't want to hear from him or know where he was. She felt the door between Jonathan and the rest of her life slam shut.

In the fall she returned to school and started her teacher training, muddling through the first semester. Bleak months followed Clare's move back from London. She wrote Jonathan one final postcard.

Three months later Lily was re-introduced to Peter Gorsky.

When she looked up, she saw Jonathan was carrying flowers, two miniature sunflowers. She felt ungenerous in her anticipation of this lunch.

"For you, and for Cynthia. I believe they were her favorite." Had he whispered it, or had it only seemed like he had? She knew now that he also had no interest in the future until they had in some way finished with the past. He was offering her a different reunion than the one she had imagined. Cynthia had always liked Jonathan.

Her eyes filled with tears and this surprised her. Too much was suddenly going on in her that she wasn't expecting. She felt happy seeing this man, although it was not a simple happiness. As if she were way back in the years when they first met, when she knew him as her friends' older brother, a foreign-looking man with bright, close-set, soft eyes, a narrow face, and long, dark hair. As if those years were inviting her now to take up the thread where it broke off. She felt young again in the company of this man whom she'd known since she was a girl. She realized she had a lot to ask him. She wanted Jonathan to tell her about his maddening disappearance. She wanted to know what happened, where he'd vanished to and where he'd been all these hidden years. She wanted to make clear, so that he understood once and finally, that she'd been right to walk away when he returned from Nicaragua. But again she hesitated, not trusting why she wanted to review this mutinous, ancient story. In her other life, the one she lived every day except this one, she cared more and more about the future. Having a child accomplished this in the most specific ways, the marking of days, the progress of weeks, Ben's day care holiday schedule on the refrigerator, the inches and hours, the next birthday party. She realized that Jonathan didn't know she'd had a child. She wondered if he had any.

JONATHAN AND LILY

He had always found her very beautiful; there had been that strong connection from the start. Her almond eyes, long lower lashes, baby hair over her upper lip, one incisor a little out of line, her strong jaw. She had been the first to make him realize how rare it was when a woman looked better undressed than dressed. But now she was even lovelier, it seemed. From what he could tell through her soft turquoise sweater and long skirt, her body had hardly changed. But her face had grown more interesting, more intriguing, more passionate in its tiny wrinkles and lines. She had freckles stretching out to her tiny heart-shaped ears and even on her eyelids. Her nostrils were two tiny crescents. He remembered the wrinkles on Lily's mother's face. She must have been about his current age when he had last seen Lucille twelve years before; now she was approaching sixty.

When she saw the sunflowers, she felt a great relief. Not that she was expecting them; he had never handed her flowers, although they were always beside the bed when she arrived in New York. Jonathan resisted gifts of all kinds. He hadn't been much for celebrating birthdays or anniversaries; he was not inclined in that way. But he had been willing to learn. She had taught him why it was important to her that he pay attention to dates, that she had certain expectations, and birthdays were important in her family. When she saw the sunflowers, she realized she had been watching for signs of wariness on his part, listening for a tone of irritation in his voice. Now she was surprised by his sweetness. She had allotted herself only an hour for lunch with him. Still, it seemed unacceptable that lunch would last only this hour and, would have to be cut short. She was scheduled to meet a colleague at one of the conference's afternoon sessions in the Pontchartrain Room, wherever that was. She carried a relief map of the entire hotel in her coat pocket. The velocity of her mind changed around Jonathan Parrish. She could barely concentrate; she was thinking too fast.

Just before he arrived, she was distracted by the sight of a young girl running her hand along the water in the fountain at the center of the lobby. The girl, perhaps six years old, was intrigued by the sheets of bright spray that came off the water as it fell from a shiny bronze statue shaped like a standing feather. She smiled watching the young girl dash along the fountain. Now she had a surge of nerves and twisted the sleeve of her sweater. She focused on objects in the restaurant to steady herself—the spiky plants, the brass lamps. Now that the running girl had disappeared, Jonathan was hard to look away from. She felt guilty, a sense of *I've been caught.* But at what? She remembered the photograph Jonathan had taken of her standing naked on his long Indonesian kitchen table in New York. She had never forgotten her first look at it. She remembered feeling pleased with her body. Her body was full and warm, her pubic hair surprisingly light and sparse, her expression one of desperate love for the man taking the picture. Accepting his flowers, gratitude returned as her pervasive emotion; it made her want to speak about the past.

Around them in the restaurant, the conventioneers talked incessantly, overflowing with good advice, singing the praises of colleagues, criticizing the pre-course speakers, insider jokes provoking applause and laughter. In the corners, old teachers sat with their former student-teachers, sipping beer. Jonathan recognized himself in the students who were a little boorish with enthusiasm as they tried to hide behind a charade of manners, but were eager to dominate the conversation with their ideas and convictions. The best of the mentors were pleased by this directness and sincerity, the stingiest unfazed, choosing the topic of conversation so they themselves could be heard. The generations represented by their mugs of beer. On one side of the table the foam collapsing, on the other side, exuberant foam bubbling over the tops of ones arriving fresh from the tap.

She had never really liked these meetings, and only went to one every few years. She didn't like being away from home, away from Ben. These meetings felt like the unnecessary but ritualized behaviors demanded by the culture of last century's teaching profession. Every presentation followed rules of delivery and organization and gave the talks a disappointing sameness. She thought of these meetings as high school reunions: the only people who went were those who felt good about themselves and their work, and wanted to brag. She had silently rebelled against these conferences, and she was aware that in part this was because they made her question how little she had accomplished. She didn't like to think of herself as one of those women teachers (the conference was three-quarters women) who bustled through the halls clutching papers and large handbags trying to find their way to the proper salon or meeting room to listen to an "expert." She instinctively distrusted experts.

When she considered his sunflowers, she was, at first, flattered that he'd done this sweet thing. Now that she reconsidered them, she was grateful in a second way. Grateful that he had released her from regret. All the complications of the past which might have jumped forward just as quickly faded away. He had always been braver than she was. It was stunning to her that he was not bitter about what she'd done to him. She looked for it in everything he'd said so far but she couldn't find a trace. How could that be? Wasn't he incredibly angry at her? How could anyone recover from what she'd done? It was remarkable. It was lovely of him to bring sunflowers. Generous. It was a way of immediately relieving any awkwardness. When she accepted them, she was convinced he was hiding no bitterness, no secret wish for revenge, no desire to make her admit to wrongdoing. He was not here to hurt.

He wanted her to have no doubts that he came not to punish her in some way, not to seek revenge, but simply to see her again. The flowers were a peace offering. She took them in her beautiful hands. Light, practical hands that knit. Veins like the tiniest embroidery. He noticed the ring. He was taken aback for a moment, but recovered quickly. His first thought was: it's a simple gold band, which is in keeping with how I remember her. Not vain, not frivolous, tasteful, direct. She wore no engagement stone, no diamond. She wore no nail polish—again, simple, without vanity. Still, he had believed, hoped, before looking at her fingers, that by now she might not be married. He held out the flowers.

"They gave me the Presidential Suite," Jonathan said, smiling, amused, breaking the silence. "Nothing to do with me. A booking error. They oversold their rooms and had nothing left except the top of the line. I could tell that the manager was a little unhappy handing over the key. It's got four or five rooms, a kitchen, glass ashtrays, chandeliers, a golden canopy over the bed. It's actually a little frightening. I don't think I've ever been in a hotel room where you couldn't stand in every corner and scan the entire room, where you weren't able to point to all that was yours. This place may be bigger than my house." She had always liked the way he just started in on a conversation, as if he had just spoken with you on this very subject five minutes before; he just said what was on his mind. And it was often surprising. He had his own take on things. When she accepted the two flowers, their fingers accidentally touched. She put the two stems in her water glass.

What she remembered as a concealed softness on his face, the small scar on his chin, was more obvious now. At twenty-two, she had considered herself vulnerable to Jonathan Parrish. The physical side had always been powerful between them—the eagerness to undress in front of him, to show him her body—it had been her refuge. It made complete sense back then, the loaded and forceful attraction she felt every time they were together. She would sit across a table from him and his eyes didn't break contact, and something halted, something paused, and it was important to remember to breathe again, to keep whatever was happening going for as long as she could. There was no reason for this feeling and she couldn't define it, but she recognized when it arrived.

She wanted to push these thoughts away as she had done for years. She had not thought of him every day for these years, not even every month, but certainly a season never went by without Jonathan surfacing in her memory.

Who could she tell about Jonathan Parrish meeting her for lunch in New Orleans? She hadn't the energy to tell Clare. She was not eager to have her comment. Years ago, her sisters had been divided on their opinions of Jonathan. Even before the end, Clare thought he represented too much of an emotional risk. What was a thirty-year-old bachelor doing with a recent college graduate? She thought Lily needed defending and was willing to go into combat for her. Cynthia understood the predicament more easily. Cynthia never minded messes. She had a certain way of registering wickedness on her face, and she got a mischievous look when she spoke about Jonathan Parrish. What would Cynthia say now if she were alive? Lily certainly couldn't call any of her friends. As she went down the list in her mind, there was a reason not to tell each and every one; this one was divorcing, that one was getting married, this one was recovering from the death of a parent. Lives complicated by their own reclamations. They were women who also knew her husband, who knew her only as part of a couple—it seemed dangerous and disloyal even when she thought of describing Jonathan as "an old friend."

She hadn't told Peter about this meal. Immediately after receiving the message in her room and deciding to invite Jonathan to lunch, she'd thought of calling her husband. But she didn't want him to object. A teenager's avoidance, not wanting to hear him say No. But when she stopped to think, she knew that if she had been casual about it, Peter wouldn't have objected to her meeting Jonathan Parrish. Her husband wasn't the jealous sort, and he never asked too many questions. Still, she hadn't reported seeing Jonathan's name in the program before she left, which would have made it easier to mention a lunch.

In a certain way, she'd felt helpless about seeing Jonathan as soon as she'd discovered him in the program, although she was not sure why. She had no wish to put her helplessness on exhibition to her husband. Maybe that was why she didn't tell him. It was too difficult to speak of any of this.

"I know that you're in Vermont, but what exactly are you doing these days?" she asked. She had some idea about his work from his articles, from the title of his featured New Orleans talk, "Children Emerging From War," but she had no sense of why he was living in a small town. This choice seemed out of keeping with what she once knew of him.

"It's not so different from the way it was before," he began. She knew that "before" meant when they were together. "I go where I'm told. But now I'm university-based. The United Nations contacts me when they need a hand. This year I only went out twice. I'm old to go out into the field, they say. It's young folks' work. They want me at a desk writing reports, but I find that awfully confining, as you can imagine. Once in awhile, if it's really important, they get the idea that I might be able to help, like with Liberia."

Her assessment had been correct twelve years before when she thought the very depths of him would never change. He valued his work above all else.

His eyes, at one moment new-leaf green, the next, tiny radial spokes colored like green glass. She wondered if he still slept in his clothes and shoes when he was on the road.

"When I'm really antsy I've got this scheme worked out. I teach members of the ministries of education in other countries. I go to Nigeria with a few junior folks and we do a monthlong course. We teach them how to set up science projects with the remnants of war. The chemistry of ash; the biology of plants that bloom in the nothingness around them; the physics of music from broken pipes, how shapes can sing. In between, I teach at the UVM, their education school. I make a little progress on a manuscript. I try to hold down a regular job.

"And what about you? I know you're in Maine, but that's about all I know."

For some reason, she hadn't expected him to ask. What man ever asked about her work? Even at a conference like this one, you could meet a man and he'd never get around to asking that single, respectful question. Still, she shouldn't have been surprised; he had always wanted to know everything she was doing, and thinking. She had no prepared answer.

"Very different from what you do. I'm in the classroom mostly. It took me a few years to get started. I was married; it seemed like too much of a bother to get an extra degree instead of just substituting, and we were living in Montana, which didn't have a program for me anyway; my husband had opened a factory up there. He didn't really like the idea of my disappearing into two or three years of homework and time away on weekends and at night." She noticed Jonathan was grinning again; she didn't remember Jonathan Parrish being this ready to smile.

Husband: the word bothered him, but he brushed it aside. He was proud of her for deciding to enter teaching. He knew she was terrific with kids. That knitting patience. Smiling was his way of silently taking credit for her becoming a teacher. He knew that he had been her model. When they were together she used to tell him that she didn't believe she was spending so much time talking about school. She'd never been much of a student in Windsor when she was the age of the children she now taught, but she got more serious in college.

When he had asked, And what about you? he had been hoping to hear something about her private life, her hopes and regrets. He realized she wasn't ready to take him there. The last twelve years was a time during which someone else had laid claim to Lily Mayeux, a part he'd never know. He felt intensely jealous for a moment. "I'm not sure that I'm hearing you're happy about your career," he said. For the second time since he sat down, she looked into his eyes and held her look.

She didn't realize how tired she was, weighted down. She had followed her husband from city to city and she was tired of work struggles, of always feeling a little behind her male colleagues, of never having accomplished enough, never getting anywhere following a straight line. Tired of scratching out the time at home to write the paper she was presenting here. One of her vice principals suggested she write about the boy in her class, Carl, with Disruptive Impulse Disorder, describing the syndrome and how it affected the classroom and her. She would be participating in a panel on "Difficult Students."

She was annoyed at herself again for agreeing to this visit with Jonathan Parrish. Already he somehow knew that she was not entirely happy with her career; he could not be fooled. What else had he figured out about her so quickly? She expected when they met to remain polite and restrained, not to talk of anything important, let alone matters of the heart. It wasn't a matter of resisting intimacies, but simply having a proper perspective on what was reasonable to expect. But now she decided to answer honestly, not to deflect, which was her habit.

"It's not exactly what I dreamed about when I started." She had never really said this before although she'd thought it plenty of times—her day was too rushed, she rarely got to spend the time she felt some of her students deserved, with the worried girl whose joints had unaccountably swollen, the boy whose father had gone to jail. But no one wanted to hear a teacher complain; people wanted you to be selfless. She wished she could be selfless, and she knew teachers who were; they still existed, and she respected them for their work habits. Jonathan, in his own way, was like this, a man who loved his work, and was devoted to it. His devotion had made it impossible for them to be together. She was sure that whatever staff he had working for him was incredibly loyal because he worked harder than any of them, staying up all night, doing whatever needed to be done. She remembered that he used to talk of her going off into the world with him, working side by side against injustice and ignorance.

Why had she answered honestly when he asked about her career? Because this reunion was remarkable and she felt grateful, and she had always told him the truth. She realized she was tired because there was nothing heavier than thinking about the past, about decisions which seemed irremediable, which felt petrified.

"My life is not exactly what I planned either, so I know what you mean," he said lightly, self-deprecatingly. "When you're on the road, you live a life where you're always telling people that you come from someplace else. By now I'm not sure where I come from."

He was surprised that she seemed a little undone, flushed, over her iced tea. Her wooly turquoise sweater seemed heavy for the New Orleans heat although the restaurant was chilled. At twenty-two, Lily had worn a blue kimono of nearly the same shade in his apartment. She would lie on her back across his bed and lift one leg up to nearly vertical, the kimono falling away, and appraise herself. She complained about her feet, the crooked toes, but he had never minded their knobbiness.

He signaled for the waitress who, he could sense, was hanging back, not wanting to interrupt. He had learned in his years away never to order from menus. Whatever the cook's specialty was for that day he accepted. In America, they made you choose from six plastic-coated pages left folded and propped against the catsup bottle; too many choices. But he was glad to see Lily order without opening a menu either, asking for gumbo. He followed her lead. He remembered her fearlessness around spices, choosing the hottest peppers, testing the reddest salsas that he brought home, a quick swig of beer to cool her throat. He was used to an empty chair opposite his; he never minded it. But company was better.

When her soup arrived, he passed her the tiny bottle of Tabasco that was hiding between the salt and pepper. "My husband thinks that by way of some strange anatomical pathway, I'm destroying brain cells whenever I eat spicy food. Even when I try cooking him the mildest curry, he screams in outrage that I'm trying to give him ulcers or ruin his sleep. I've pretty much given up trying." Jonathan Parrish had taught her about spices, bringing in mysterious roots and plants and syrups from the tiny New York shops near his apartment. His taste for the exotic hadn't matched up with the cereal he ate every morning from bright red and green boxes, his Cap'n Crunch and Lucky Charms, or the newest kid-brand he saw advertised on television. The milk turned yellow and he would lift the bowl to his lips and drink the final honeyed drops. His cereal assessments were nuanced, and she wondered now whether this special pleasure of his was one of the reasons she never felt like she was too young for him.

Jonathan Parrish was the forgotten trail to her childhood. His message this afternoon drove her mind back to the tiny village in Connecticut, her family home, the home of her parents, both of whom he'd known. Today, just hearing Jonathan's voice, after years of not knowing what had become of him, made her miss her home, although of course she no longer knew what was happening there, her mother dead two years now, her father having moved away, nearer to his sister in North Carolina, then dying suddenly three months ago. Jonathan Parrish was the lost man returning after years of wandering, and he was *her* return. Before last night, she never realized she had a yearning to be reminded of Windsor. Deep inside her, he created a longing, although she was not entirely sure what for. He had provoked in her a desire for absent things. Still, or perhaps *because* of these feelings, she'd felt the need to mention her husband.

The ring on her long finger holding her iced tea. In those first years apart, Jonathan liked to believe that if she married, her marriage to someone else wouldn't last. But it obviously had. He didn't want to think about this right then. "Can you help me with my speech while we eat? I haven't quite finished it yet, and I haven't done a talk like this before. An audience outside my oddball field. Did you know I'm here to give a speech?" He gave a quick glance, smiled slightly, unsure, suddenly a little shy after this outpouring. Lily had had a keen eye for cliché, and she could help his talk—really just notes, although his performance was four hours away—before he got up there and bored people.

"Yes, I know why you're here," she said, teasing, light, "you're on stage in four hours." She thought: Isn't everybody aware that you're speaking today? Your name is the bold one listed as the first speaker on today's opening program. He'd put his black shoulder bag down beside his chair. He leaned over to open its simple flap, and mumbled sorting through the bag's contents. It was a battered pocket of leather that had been to a lot of dusty places over the years. Looking at it, she could tell that Jonathan Parrish appreciated age and patina, not flashiness. He had a sense of value, that everything had a history and he didn't throw things out. She could see a shirt folded inside. Stuffed into the pockets were identical silver-capped pens. She noticed a guidebook for New Orleans.

He removed a red folder. "I used a folder like this as a rain hat once. In the car that day, I put it on my lap as I was being driven to meet the Minister of Gambia. The color ran. I ruined a good pair of pants."

She could tell he enjoyed telling this story on himself, his lack of foresight, his ridiculous bad luck. She could imagine Jonathan in clogs and stained pants sitting down unembarrassed with the leader of an African nation. "But still you use a red folder," she said. Her voice sounded strange, as if it belonged to someone else. There was noise in the restaurant that she wanted to make go away.

She noticed his hands were small as he reached for his bag again, but that his fingers were long. She had always liked his hands. His nose, tipped down, was a little crooked, complicated-looking. His lips were full, dry. He looked tired, or perhaps he was simply older. He pulled out a pen. "I try to stay out of the rain," he said. "Can I get your advice on this?"

To organize her racing mind, she ran down a list of friends and acquaintances attending this meeting, scanned the tables around them and outside beyond the glass windows. Most of them, as far as she knew, were doing what they always did: circulating, sitting in on the sessions in the smaller galleries, networking. What she usually forced herself to do, but wasn't doing today. She thought of her father saying, "Lily, why do you have to be the one?"

She worked through the first pages of his talk with him, making minor suggestions about what she thought the audience would be familiar with and what they wouldn't have heard of. He had been almost relieved to have something to concentrate on and talk about with her. There were so many subjects that felt off-limits.

Lily Mayeux had always been bold. He wondered what she had in mind inviting him to lunch. He wondered what he had in mind accepting.

"Oh, not now," he said, closing the red folder. "What a ridiculous way to spend my little time with you." He told her he'd driven twenty-four straight hours. He apologized for being dusty. When he stood to take off his jacket she could see the dark circles under his arms.

When he looked at her bowl, he noticed she'd eaten almost nothing after nearly an hour, a few bites from her gumbo. "You have an appointment?" he asked. "I don't want to keep you."

She assumed he was finished eating and needed some time alone to polish his words. She watched the muscles in his forearm flex as he put his pen away. Still, it felt abrupt, his decision to end their lunch. After an hour of talk, she felt unraveled. She didn't want lunch to end. She considered how unusual it had been, an hour speaking privately with a man other than her husband—when did that ever happen? She wanted to know more about his answer to the one question that had maddened her twelve years before: Why had it taken weeks to call after her telegrams to Nicaragua? She could feel her face grow warm. He rose slowly, gently.

She had wanted to keep the conversation simple and superficial. After all these years there was no right thing to say to him about what happened years before, why she had ended things so abruptly, without a conversation, without an explanation, sending him only a single postcard? And now they were virtual strangers, weren't they?—brought together by accident.

Today, Jonathan Parrish made her feel lonely. Lonely for what? For what was gone? For what she'd turned her back on?

"Do you know where the speaker preparation room is? If you'd like me to show you, I actually passed it. It's way off in the corner of the hotel," she said.

"I don't need to get ready yet. Anyway, I'd rather take a walk around the neighborhood. Clears my head. I always walk before I talk. If you have the time, would you like to join me?"

"I have the time," she said. "I need to make one stop before we go. Will you excuse me?"

He took a small drink of his coffee and watched her. A pretty face, a lovely body—his first glance was correct—surprisingly unchanged, from what he could tell. But there were compelling women everywhere. The young researchers at the university; the education department administrators in Kentucky and Colorado and Mozambique. Still, there had always been an intense physical attraction to Lily. Chemistry, she called it. But it was like no chemistry that he had ever studied; you'd need a separate atomic theory for why two people couldn't keep their hands off one another. As she walked away, he tried to see her more clearly from a distance. She was as tall and startling as a woman painted by Masaccio. Her long legs carried her in perfect balance, her hips swung as she walked, but her wide shoulders barely swayed at all. She was still above the waist. There rose before his mind a vivid picture of her mother. Did Lily see the resemblance? She had the brow and bend of her mother's head. He wondered if he looked much older to her. He would trust her as a far better judge than a mirror.

In the ladies' room she chastised herself for being too hard on his speech. Hadn't he once told her that he'd become a "traveling teacher" so that he would not have a real boss? He worked only for himself and his students. In the mirror, she saw her eyes were alive. At the corners of her mouth were wrinkles, but fine ones that didn't dishearten her. Her body had changed little since he knew her, even with the birth of her son. On her wrist was a gold bracelet of linked gingko leaves her mother had given her. Her mother had always had an unexpected soft spot for Jonathan, she remembered, from the little they had discussed him.

Jonathan Parrish's movements were subtle and subdued, minimal, understated. His sentences trailed off into mumbles and were completed by a pursing of his lips, a delicate shrug, a mild widening of his eyes. There had always been a light in Jonathan Parrish's eyes, a sort of invitation. His eyes said: "Let's be young together. Let's see things for the first time and tell each other the absolute truth, want to?" She wanted to ask him if he had children, if he had ever married, but she wasn't ready to hear the answers. She tried to remember if they ever fought in the old days. They must have—over one or another disagreement—but she couldn't remember any specific instances.

On her way back to the table, she stopped at a hotel phone to leave a message in the room of the woman she was to meet after lunch. She saw Jonathan pacing just outside the restaurant entrance. He wore his black bag over his right shoulder. The little girl who had been playing near the fountain an hour before was making another winding path through the lobby, her arms out like airplane wings. She came dashing toward Jonathan who caught himself mid-stride so as not to trample her. As the girl passed by, he leaned over to touch her golden hair very gently, which the child didn't seem to notice at first, then looked back at him charmingly on her way somewhere else.

At twenty-two, Lily had a bored, irritable quality at times, a moodiness. He tried to trick her into admissions of enthusiasm, into expressions of pure happiness. It was a game. Today, she seemed subdued, but there was no need for games. He had never expected to be comforted by her (that's why the days after his appendectomy were such a surprise), and he wasn't expecting it now.

He had recently read about a phenomenon called speed dating. Forty or fifty men and women met in a bar or community center and rotated through seven-minute dates with one another. A bell rang, breaking the couples up and moving each dater on to a new seven-minute partner. Cost-effective, urgent, wasteless matchmaking. Name tags, dim lights, score sheets like bingo cards with spaces for age, race, religion. Flirting boot camp, one woman had called it. A life story in a minute-and-a-half. What he had with Lily seemed exactly the opposite of speed-dating. There were so many questions to ask her. About her mother, her father, her sisters. And of course: How was she able to turn away from him?

She welcomed the walk and the fresh air. They moved through the revolving front door of the hotel into the southern humidity, and she asked, "Which way?" When Jonathan turned to look to his left, she glanced at his profile. His chin was cocked. He wasn't handsome in any conventional sense, but she'd always liked the way he looked. Thin, lithe, streamlined, he was built for speed, yet his pace was leisurely. His body rejected anything that might weigh him down. Their strides matched perfectly; she remembered that.

He drew the street guide from his black bag. He had always loved maps. They could occupy him for hours. All the coded information about space and distance packed onto a single page. It was the simplification and abstraction of the landscape that appealed so much. When he was little he liked to follow along the map as his father drove, correlating it with what he saw out the windows. Now he simply liked to figure out where he was and how to get where he was going, especially if he had to use features like where the road curved, a stream, or the angle at which streets met to solve the puzzle, things which weren't labeled, but that reflected relationships. He always felt that if he were lost, he'd be in his element.

"How long do you think your talk will be?" she asked.

"Are you trying to decide whether to attend?" He smiled.

She suddenly remembered when she'd gotten rid of any evidence of Jonathan's presence in her life; his letters, books they'd shared, a sweater he'd loaned her. It was the day of her first wedding anniversary.

A walk after lunch, one of her favorite activities, but one she hadn't done in years, maybe since her last conference, the last time she'd spent two days away from her family. On weekdays, after a twenty-minute lunch at her desk, she went right back to work, making calls to parents, completing paperwork, in order to get home by three-thirty. On weekends, she took her son to the park (recently they'd gently watered worms there; Ben convinced himself they were overheated), or if Ben napped, she caught up on housework. They were planning to put in a new kitchen. That meant a million decisions—lighting, counters, drawer pulls, appliances, a new gas line. Should the cabinets have a crown molding? This walk was a luxury.

She removed her sweater and tied the sleeves around her waist. She wore a black, sleeveless blouse. Her shoulders were bony, clearly outlined. He noticed her toenails were painted a silvery-purple. In the old days, she would have considered any polish vain, and he was delighted that she took care of herself now in this small way.

Why had he contacted her? They might have both attended this large meeting and simply missed one another. But how often did one get a chance to ask an old lover about the far-off past? Watching her nails in their sandals, and the jutting bones of her ankles, he was reminded of the urge to reach her, to drive faster the night before, as he crossed into Louisiana, smoking a full pack between the Louisiana border and the New Orleans city limits, slowing only to finish his last pear. The more he thought about what had happened the more he could understand her astonishing behavior twelve years before. By remaining in

Nicaragua as long as he did, he had misbehaved. "Misbehaved" was one of his self-protective words, his minimizing excuse.

There had been no large or spectacular fight with her—he was too stunned, she had disappeared—so that the deep damage was never revealed. Not in the wildest realm of possibility did he consider his time would end with Lily the way that it had. Everything they had and were together simply changed over a few weeks.

Only now, as he studied her beautiful shoulders, did he face the truth that what he had told himself and his brothers and anyone else who asked over the years—that he couldn't make it back to the States in time for Cynthia's funeral—was only a half-truth. He stayed in Nicaragua for the reason he went in the first place: it was his work he loved most. He stayed for the children, but he also stayed for himself. Believing Lily would take him back when he returned. He hated himself for this mistake.

He had been in the jungle when her telegram arrived reporting that Cynthia had died. He should have hurried to Managua and flown to Connecticut. But he didn't. He stayed in the steamy mountains, a crazy man finishing the work he'd started, tempting fate. He had never had the chance to explain this selfish, indefensible blunder. He tried calling when he returned to the States three weeks later, but her father had never put him through to Lily. But what could he have said, anyway? Nothing that would have been adequate, he understood now. By the time he returned to the United States, one part of his life had ended and another began.

She saw that he noticed her toenails. She'd chosen a silver, slightly lavender, summery polish. Her son had suggested either green or silver and she had gone down the grooming path toward a motorcycle-chrome shade a four-year-old was sure to admire.

In the French Quarter, Jonathan appreciated the turn-of-the-century government buildings with their marble staircases, and groaning cage elevators you could see through the open front doors. She noticed the homes that had sunken courtyards with dense vegetation in the back, visible down thin alleys. In some ways, he wasn't at all as she expected. She realized she had been worried that Jonathan would be difficult, that he would pressure her, ask hard questions and be dissatisfied with her answers, a reflection of his too-high expectations of others. But, he spoke little about himself. He seemed more humble than she remembered, more careful in his dealings with the human race. She considered telling him these impressions as they walked. There were so many questions to ask him; what did she really know to ask when she was twenty-two? She wanted to know about his mother, his father, his brothers. But they were quiet in the noise of the side streets, crowded and commercial, the smoke shops and boulangeries and voodoo emporia, the honking trucks and men carrying Louis XIV antiques on their shoulders. Tourists moved slowly as stores closed for their long, late lunches. It smelled like she remembered France smelled, dark and damp, the mixed scents of old drains, burnt wood, cat piss. Ancient and secret. Garlic and oil and cologne. The one trip she had taken abroad with Jonathan, they had stayed in a brick villa in Lyons with black-painted window frames and kittens who hid under inverted flowerpots. They ate outdoors where waiters came to sing to them. They left half-finished cups of coffee and wine at cafés so they could get back indoors. She curled her body between his legs, exploring with her mouth. Later, joined at the waist, he would lift his chest off hers and look with incredible wonder and curiosity, like he was amazed she was there at all. In red robes, they went out to the balcony and filled themselves with the bougainvillea scent of late afternoon, and waited for the silhouettes of distant mountains to grow sharper at dusk.

New Orleans was a city of war veterans and cannons from Napoleonic times and wrought iron like Lyons, of geraniums in planters, of sweet girls blowing kisses and cops saluting, a city that emitted a sense of triumph. A city where Jonathan again seemed amazed that she had materialized.

The past was part of today, the walk, being with Lily again. Years before, had they ever gotten to talking about how life would be someday, how they would be? Had they ever wandered together more than a few weeks into the future? There was always planning the next visit back then to absorb them. He often wondered, over the years, how it would have been different, living with Lily. It would have been different from their year together, but he did not know how.

"Do you have any children?" he asked. She balked for a moment, wasn't sure she'd heard him right, he said it so softly. Although it was a question anyone might ask in getting to know her, coming from Jonathan it seemed almost too intimate, and for a moment she didn't want to answer.

"Yes," she answered, "one." Slightly short of breath, immediately needing to change the subject.

He didn't pursue the details of her family life when he saw she found it difficult to continue. If she wanted to tell him more she would. For the same reason he had not expected her marriage to last, he was surprised to hear she had a child. Lily was quiet. He looked over at her from time to time as they walked. She was thirty-five with delicate features, a classic nose, a long neck of spare simplicity. Muted but powerful signals stirred in him. They proceeded out of the dark avenues of the Quarter toward the river embankment, the sun a hammer. The clouds looked like a plowed field. The brown water flowed quickly where the Mississippi formed an elbow. A ferry carrying a few people slid slowly toward them from a platform on the far shore, moving sidewise insect-like, resisting the current. He spotted something that caught his interest down by the water and scampered down over the gravel.

He moved with unwasted motion toward the river. He had long legs and he brushed his hair with both hands once he reached his stopping point. She looked away for a moment, studying the progress of the ferry, and when she looked back, he was squatting on a rock near the water. At the shoreline she could see clearly the shape of the earth and color of the sky. It made her nervous when he turned to her again, his face serious. Then he waved and stood. He returned holding out a small bouquet of wild flowers that mixed well with the two sunflowers she held in her left hand. She felt something thump at the bottom of her throat as she remembered his New York neighborhood and its windowboxes of impatiens. The birds flying up from the streets of northern Manhattan, the coolness of the chapel's stones on 172nd street, the subway entrance at 168th like a yawning cistern, the enormous eyes of the Dominican children and the neatly dressed Haitian couples on Sunday mornings.

She asked about his brothers.

"Harry's a man with a belly and the invented symptoms of middle age, and Paul spends a lot of time at his desk," Jonathan explained. "They have two teenaged children apiece, and all four of them like malls too much."

From what he'd told her of Burlington at lunch, she imagined Jonathan Parrish in a small, low-ceilinged cottage facing Lake Champlain, the last in a row of cottages down an unpaved road. It was autumn, and the living room—maybe the whole house was one large room with an open kitchen—had a spluttering fire and a few chairs, a couch facing the window, looking out at the water. There was a bicycle leaning against the front gate, and a garden of ferns and small conifers covering the front yard just to the edge of where the property sloped down to the black-stoned beach. Tall pines shaded it cool and damp, with pebbles in the driveway that never quite dried.

There was something alive in his eyes, a buried rage, a kind of hope. As he spoke about his family, she drifted. It was easy to fall into the old life of memory. She struggled to resist the past. She did not want it to reclaim her totally.

His speech was brief, eccentric, and funny. There was an energy to it, a power, evidence of a fast mind. It was a verbal exhibition of the way she knew he worked, imposing his will, dominant, using skill and intellect and charm. He had put on a clean khaki shirt in their hour apart. He was probably the only speaker they'd ever invited who didn't wear a tie, she thought.

Lost on paper when she'd started to read them in the restaurant, he had invigorated four or five case studies with the heat of a live performance. When Jonathan spoke, he had none of the professional heaviness of voice one expected listening to public speakers. He talked about confronting and shaping the aftermath of war for the sake of children. He made clear how everywhere he went parents would do anything for their children except stop fighting. He offered examples of how he tried to mobilize this parental attention and affection to build schools. He admitted to mistakes and missteps in places he "didn't know well enough." He spoke of his now famous idea of sending mothers to school with their children (she remembered him thinking of this twelve years before in his apartment, that educating women would prevent disease). He shared tales of great hope and despair. He spoke of the power of rice throughout the world, its many possible uses in math and science and history teaching. She laughed like everyone else, and thought of the single mother of one of her students, a sweet, romantic woman who carried around a box of rice, "waiting for a wedding." The woman had tossed a few grains at Lily's feet after her visit that week. Even if you didn't know Jonathan, it was obvious from his talk that he had a hobo persona. In the slides he showed you could see he barely brought along clothes; he slept under chaises; he had a subversive quality, a contempt for authority and the normal way of doing things.

But he was serious; he described exotic places in terms of the suffering of thousands. She remembered the younger Jonathan complaining about his colleagues' attitudes toward traveling. They were oblivious to their surroundings. "They only want to get there, do their job, and get home."

She tried to think of all she secretly knew of Jonathan Parrish, all the things this audience would never know. Certain things could not be touched by time: his eyes, his voice, the way he touched the top of his head when he was nervous. But he was different too. Some of his restlessness was gone. His face seemed less capable of hardness than she remembered. Something shifted in her, something she hadn't noticed at lunch: more of Jonathan Parrish, that's what she wanted.

At times, she couldn't look at him, even from thirty rows back; he was too much to take in. Sitting in the dark as he showed his slides to two thousand teachers, she realized that before, time was made of what was past and she marked it backward to when she was a small girl. Today, it felt like time should be measured by how much of the future she had left, and needed to be counted forward. She felt proud listening, as if somehow Jonathan Parrish's speech reflected on her, as if she could take credit for some part of it, for him.

After the speech, she stayed just outside the crowd that had gathered around him in front of the podium. He took questions patiently. She could tell he was exhausted, something he never admitted even after coming in from ten time zones away; she remembered the surest sign of his fatigue was his ability to fall asleep on his back, when most nights he slept on his stomach, one knee pulled toward his chest.

He reached through the wall of questioners and gently pulled her inside the circle. "This is my colleague, Lily Mayeux. She will be giving a wonderful talk tomorrow morning about how best to teach the most difficult of difficult children, and you all must attend."

With this recommendation, they turned to her and began to ask the name and place of her session.

When everyone was gone, she said, "A talk like that will make everyone run out and have rice for dinner."

"And they probably should."

"Can I cook you dinner in the Presidential Suite? Let me show you what I've learned in the past twelve years," she said. The words were out of her mouth before she could think about them.

"That sounds wonderful. Might as well make use of the kitchen. I've eaten too many meals in diners in the last twenty-four hours; I'm ready for something new, that's for sure. But don't go to much trouble."

"The suite has silverware and pans and an oven?"

"Yes it does."

"Could I come by at 7?" she asked. "It will take me a little while to get organized."

She went shopping in the Quarter—they'd passed a farmers market and a few gourmet food shops on their walk earlier—for onions and cheese and pistachios in their shells, for Gulf shrimp and cappellini and ginger and cream. She bought tatsoi greens and red peppers, watercress and olive oil. Back at her room, she took the ice bucket and filled it with cubes from the machine down the hall, and planted all the spoilables in the ice.

In Maine, it was past dinnertime and Ben would be eager to hear from her. When Peter answered the phone, she felt impatient to hear her son's squeaky voice. "How was Ben's doctor appointment today?" she asked.

"He wouldn't let anyone touch him. He screamed and kicked and yelled." Peter sounded exasperated. "We rescheduled."

She knew this tantrum was about her going away and she felt badly; she always took Ben to his appointments. "That's okay. He's healthy. We'll go another time."

"To calm him afterward, I took him for ice cream." This was a surprise. Her husband didn't usually reward "bad" behavior and she was delighted. "But he dripped chocolate syrup on his shirt. It's probably ruined." Peter said it in a way that implied he wouldn't make the mistake of offering such a treat again.

She recalled a night earlier in the week when Ben had been devoured by mosquitoes, leaving his ankles red and itchy. She had filled a pasta pot of soapy water, elevated it on two phone books, and put him in a rocking chair to watch TV. In his bathrobe, with a bowl of ice cream on his lap, he looked like an 80-year-old with sore feet.

Ben got on the phone and told her about his Dalmatian doll, then quickly handed the receiver back to his father. Lily felt irritated by her husband's upset and at the same time sorry for him; why couldn't he just enjoy the boy? Two days alone with his son, and Ben was such a good boy. When Peter got back on the line she felt she had something to confess, but again she wasn't sure what she would say, and thought: better just leave it alone right now. They went over the time of her flights. She told him about the heat and the carved chairs in the antique store windows on Royal Street. She'd bought a gift for Ben—a pink and purple-feathered voodoo figure—but she couldn't figure out what to buy for her husband. Even after all these years she wasn't sure if he'd like pralines.

When he got back upstairs, Jonathan lit a cigarette. The suite was fine even if it made him a little uncomfortable with its luxuries. When a foreign government put him up he never minded the apartments they gave him, far less grand than this hotel, rented rooms with rented furniture, somebody's image of what Westerners might like. He carried his few keepsakes and that was enough to make a room in Burma feel comfortable. When he had returned to New York after Lily disappeared, he tried to stave off despair. He loved New York, its streets were his, its sounds were always a pleasure to his ear, but without her and the domesticity they'd shared, he felt as if he were back in Central America, in exile; to escape, he accepted every available foreign assignment he was offered.

He inspected the kitchen of the Presidential Suite more thoroughly. There was cutlery, but no dishes, he discovered. He took the elevator back down and went out again into the Quarter to buy beer and a bottle opener and plastic plates. Wandering, he also found a small package of dried alligator meat, which he bought as a joke, a contribution to the dinner she was planning. When he got back to the suite, he drank one of the Delta beers he picked up—he always tried the local products.

To calm herself, she took up her knitting and sat in the wingback chair near the window in her room. What was it about their time together in New York? she wondered. The privacy, the "we're alone in the world" feeling inside his apartment? Those moments when she was immodest with him, when she would brush his pants and he would get hard in an instant, when she worshipped the shape of his head, the click of his teeth, the back of his neck, his smell? Jonathan would always put the purple freesia in a vase on her side of the bed before she arrived. She woke up full of happy energy, with a tingling contentment, woke up hungry for the sight of him.

She enjoyed the softness of the new yarn and how it immediately produced in her a sensation of unconcern. But the real reasons she loved knitting were more mathematical. She liked the structure and simplicity with which knitting produced something two- or three-dimensional out of something one-dimensional. She had described this to friends many times: Imagine a row of loops on a knitting needle—imagine just wrapping the yarn around and around the needle like a spiral. Now you were going to put another row of loops through that first row of loops. You approached the first loop. You could put another loop through it either by pulling the new one through from the back, so that the top of the old loop was in back of the new loop (knit) or you could pull the new one through from the front, so that the top of the old one was in front of the new one (purl). That's it. That's all there was to it. (There were a few other things, like knitting two stitches together to make one, or turning one stitch into two, or making an extra loop on the needle, but they were really elaborations of the basic knit and purl.) It appealed to her that it was so simple. It was like the idea of natural selection—just extremely simple—but look at what beautiful things you could make!

She remembered, early on, looking into his empty refrigerator (eggs, milk, butter, three beers) and wondering what he ate. This was before she'd seen him cook in the apartment's large kitchen. When she visited, they spent much of their time at the long, worn teak table, pots boiling on the stove. On the windowsill that faced an airshaft, herbs grew in clay pots. While he cooked—Thai fish cakes, Moroccan stews—he would study bound reports marked CONFIDENTIAL, and she would read Tolstoy, and they would both intermittently stand to wash the pans he dirtied. He brought in ingredients she had never seen before from tiny Asian markets, from Central American mercados where he knew the owners. He had an iron stomach. This was when she first understood that cooking was about sex, sensual in the same way.

The Indonesian table had two long benches and she remembered the way she would straddle the seat and he would copy her so that she could lean against him, not really breathing, his chest against her back. In loving him, she had never been able to help herself. She'd been unembarrassed when he'd asked her to take off her clothes and step onto the table that day. He moved around below her, using the camera he had drawn from his closet, shooting up at her. He turned her admiringly. All the parts of her body that she might have hidden, she flaunted because it pleased him. Her rebellious heart beat fast. She hadn't cared who might ever see these photographs, or what they'd think. All her time alone with him was filled with such unconcern. "You are a feast of love," he kept telling her, smiling. And she believed it around him, although she had never really considered herself beautiful. Sometimes he would stop and set aside the camera and just stare at her. She remembered seeing her pale nipples in his photographs and being delighted by them. She had never posed on a table again, for him or anyone else.

She was no longer a girl of twenty-two. She was a woman in her mid-thirties, focused, private. Jonathan understood; he had called her his "colleague;" she was grateful, flattered.

As she looked out the window on the twelfth floor, she wondered what it required not to be afraid. After a few hours with Jonathan Parrish he had the run of her imagination. It was almost more than she could deal with. She recalled that Jonathan had given her the key to his apartment so she could go there whenever she wanted, even when he was away. It was very convenient at the time, when she was angry with a roommate and needed to be out of Hartford for a day or two. Jonathan used to paint in his spare time and she remembered the smell of his drying oils. At home, in the late afternoon, he would put an easel out on the fire escape and paint to the shadowy sounds of pigeons coming and going, hat tops and bald spots and stickball games on the street below his odd, elevated perch. She inspected his canvases when he was gone. Did he still paint? Did he still play hockey? She had a million questions to ask him. They used to lie in bed, their bare limbs crossed, and discuss small pleasures. He liked dark and airy bedrooms, windows on three sides, shades down. He liked a light cover on a summer night; waking up a little cold to find another blanket was perfect. He liked almonds, skinned and blanched, and dried apricots. He liked to drive fast on highways at night with the radio loud. It was strange all she'd forgotten and now remembered.

He showered. He'd thought of Lily Mayeux regularly over the years, but after the first few years only within certain stable limits. This afternoon, moments from their year together rushed forward and what a few years before had seemed weightless now took on mass, and oscillated with huge meaning. She was married, but was it to the same man she had married in the months after Cynthia's death, a fellow college student, according to his brothers who provided him with information from old friends in Windsor? He hadn't thought about her husband since lunch and didn't want to start now; he wanted to concentrate on Lily. How had having a child changed her?

On this day of reunion, it was easy to idealize her. There must have been moments, during that year twelve years before, when she wanted to be together and he wanted to be alone, moments of misunderstanding and frustration, when conversation went off in the wrong direction toward blame, and unfair things were said, when tiredness showed, but he couldn't remember them.

As she approached the corner door to the Presidential Suite, she remembered how she explained their split to friends back then: The geometry of Jonathan's life was unable to contain her. "You're not the third-world kind, sleeping outside in rainstorms," was how Clare put it. At the time, she couldn't guess what pain she had caused, but it was there, she knew, from the moment he sent his last letter. On their walk in the French Quarter what had happened years before had not been brought up. He'd been patient, and had not said a word. Another kindness. Because he had been kind, it made her feel kind, less tense.

Part 3: Friday Evening

LILY AND JONATHAN

When he opened the door, he traded an opened bottle of Delta for one of the bags of groceries she carried. As he stooped to cradle the supplies, she kissed him on the forehead, barely a touch. He looked up only enough to see her smile softly, but not enough to meet her eyes. He wanted to stand straight and kiss her back, on the lips. Don't, Jonathan warned himself. She was not here for anything like that. But then he thought: maybe Paul was right, maybe I have been waiting for Lily Mayeux. He'd never really accepted this before; he presumed that Paul, in his own way, had just been pointing out how difficult it was to make him happy, how he really didn't give the women he'd been with a chance.

"You must spend half your life in hotel rooms," she said, following him down the hallway.

"Not like this," he said. Did he mean, this size room, or not with a woman, not with her? With one shoulder, he pushed in the swinging door to the kitchen and they each put their bags down on the formica counter. The kitchen was uninterrupted white, laboratory-esque, the window, facing another wing of the hotel, without a curtain, the metal cabinets slightly dented, the white stove top scratched in places. Only a cigarette burn on the table's surface gave the room a feeling of previous occupants. This time she brought the flowers, dahlias, bursts of light beautifully symmetric, red and orange and pink fireworks. "I find that the one little flaw in them is the thing that makes a flower interesting," he said as he filled his empty bottle with water and used it as a vase.

At home, she rarely drank alcohol, but at conferences she sometimes went out with friends in the evening. She felt odd accepting this beer from him, but not enough to deny herself. "Are you always this friendly with strangers, letting them invite themselves for dinner? Is that the Vermont way?" she asked flirtatiously. She worried that she wasn't going to be able to resist what had been put in her path; she had been unable to keep a clear mental picture of Peter all day, even during her call home; she didn't want to hurt him. The demands and vows and rigors of marriage seemed far away and she tried to pull them closer. Why had Jonathan Parrish not answered her telegrams before Cynthia's funeral had passed? And if he had appeared in Windsor that day would they still be together? How easily life was one thing and not another.

"You can tell strangers anything," he answered. He repeated his reminder to himself: she is a stranger—I don't know a single detail from her life of the last decade. But Lily was also incredibly familiar. Although he had not seen her in years, after these few hours he felt he could tell her anything. Once upon a time, they had had a typical life: a morning newspaper, a juice maker, Correlli on the stereo in New York, the city of their romance, where she'd insisted she would live some day. He remembered her excitedly telling him she would join AmeriCorps Teachers and request a posting in Washington Heights so they could live together. They almost never wore clothes in private. Her skin appeared polished. She would sway and rub her arms and rock on her heels and talk. Seeing her, it all came back so quickly. He felt as if the nights they had together never ended, as if there was still a continuous unbroken string of nights. He was alive in a real and complete way for the first time in years.

"Need help?" he asked.

She held the configuration of the Parrish's kitchen in her mind perfectly. She never thought of dating Jonathan in those days; he was eight years older and gone from the house, while she had the typical tomboy dilemmas. But she had always loved walking into the Parrish family house in Windsor, becoming suddenly immersed in its great laughing chatter. The fat orange cat, Alice, that would rub against anyone; one or another boy bouncing a ball off a wall or sliding glass door somewhere; a trumpet being practiced upstairs. All the plants, the aquarium, the birdcage high above Alice's reach. All the cabinets in the kitchen open as if someone had just pulled out a cup or a plate to help themselves to food and left the cupboards available for the next person, or because they'd soon be back for more. Jonathan's father kept the house at sauna temperature and told her off-color jokes, a ten-year-old boy's sense of humor. With bright blue suspenders and bright blue eyes, with white hair and wide gestures, he welcomed you as if you were a plane pulling up to his gate.

She thought of Jonathan's father canning and bottling fruits and vegetables. From when she was ten to maybe fifteen, she was invited over every autumn for pickling, joining Paul, who was in her homeroom year after year, and Harry around the butcher block table in the kitchen. There would be a giant tin washbasin of cucumbers on the floor that they had collected from the trellis in the backyard that morning. Everyone would get a newly sharpened knife and a large white apron, and would get to work shaving the "fruits," as Jonathan's father called them. Mrs. Parrish would prepare the Ball jars, sterilizing them on the stove, a range with six flame burners. They would prop a giant chalk board on the counter by the window and when a cucumber was peeled, you would mark it with a slash on the board. You could watch the progress in groups of five with their slanting chalk lines. With the cukes peeled, the entire family would engage in a debate over how many jars of dill and how many jars of sour and how many of sweet they should bottle. Paul always voted for dill only. Lily preferred the bread and butters because they could soak unsterilized in the giant glazed earthenware containers that were so exotic. Mr. Parrish cast the deciding vote. Then the brines would be prepared.

She shook her head and walked past Jonathan to the refrigerator, feeling his eyes on her back for the second time in a day, wondering if she looked the same to him, guessing that she didn't, perhaps a little wider, but reasonably close (her son had been a small baby and she hadn't put on much weight during her pregnancy), hoping that she was still attractive to him. She'd noticed that his body had changed some too; his legs were even thinner, as if he'd been on the move for twelve years. On the counter he'd laid out what he kept in his pockets: keys, his wallet, a piece of hotel writing paper folded to a quarter of its size and covered with jottings, a few jacks, a superball, the stub of a pencil, a fireball candy. He had always filled his pockets like a young teenager. The first time she'd made note of this, he told her, "Life's too serious not to carry a yo-yo."

It seemed miraculous that he'd found her. What were the chances? She added up the improbables. He hadn't given a large public talk in years. She rarely went to conferences. He was invited to speak to a group of general educators, an audience he'd never faced before, rather than to other international policy makers. She hadn't changed her last name. He happened to read the program before leaving, including the list of attendees. It had taken all these chance happenings to push him toward her again. She knew coincidence spoke to him; Jonathan believed fortuity always held a message and was significant.

"You don't need help?" he asked skeptically. "This one's all yours?" He seemed disappointed.

"Don't you think I owe you?" she said, and paused, but decided not to make too much of any debts. "After all the meals you cooked for me."

"That was a long time ago," he said.

She relented. "You can be my sous-chef. Come peel the shrimp, you." She said it in a mock-bossy tone.

They met at the refrigerator where he grabbed the bag of shrimp and she took out the vegetables. He had always been comfortable in the kitchen, always seemed to have the right supplies and implements. He took a covered blade from his pocket which he switched open and washed off in the sink. He laid it on the counter so she could cut the tomatoes and celery.

"How long will you be here?" she asked, looking down at the piles she was creating on the countertop.

"Probably just two days. I was planning on driving back tomorrow or the following day. I have some chores to do around my house, in my vegetable garden, and I'm working up a class I'm planning to teach in the fall."

She was surprised to hear he had a garden; her mental picture of his life in Vermont was bound to be wrong. A garden meant he'd settled down somewhere at some point, spent a whole season in one place, or at least enough time to plant and fertilize and water and weed. A garden seemed like a project that was too slow for him.

A garden meant time when he wasn't working. She had never known him to take four hours off, to relax. He was productive in that way of ambitious men, men who really didn't have time for relationships that required tending. He had not called for weeks after Cynthia's death; even in love, she understood that this level of self-absorption, or whatever it was, was unacceptable. A garden, another surprise.

"There was a woman I was with some years ago who kept a large garden." He could see Lily stiffen slightly. "She grew rhubarb and Swiss chard and asparagus and three kinds of lettuce. She knew her stuff. She would go out to the farms near where we lived and bring in manure to lay around the raspberries. She sent away for seeds from fancy catalogs and started them in cups in the basement under bright lights. We planted a fig tree and even an olive tree. She wanted to feed us for half a year completely from her growings. We lasted together through three gardens. Never married, wisely."

"Never married." The way he said it, she assumed he meant: not to the gardener nor anybody else. She wondered why he never married the Swiss chard lady, but she didn't ask. She presumed there had been other women. She felt the asymmetry though: she was married and he wasn't.

She hadn't had much experience around the kitchen when he knew her, but now she obviously did. She fumbled a little, but he knew it was out of nervousness. Neither of them was a fearless, ceaseless talker, and she asked if there was a radio in the Presidential Suite. Since lunch, in his mind, images had blinked on unexpectedly, abruptly, swiftly, and gone out instantly. It wasn't exactly daydreaming, because he hadn't tried to bring them on. Just quiet, contented memories. She brushed his arm and suddenly his old backyard in Windsor rose up before him for a split second. She turned her head in a certain way and he instantly recognized her ice skating on the pond behind his house. She touched the dahlias in their vase and he remembered her family's garden which was little more than a few marigolds. Ever since Lily arrived these fleeting images visited him and assuaged his longing.

Chopping, she stood two feet from him. She was suddenly conscious that she was in a hotel room with Jonathan Parrish. She considered ways to keep the conversation neutral.

"I really don't know if there's a radio," he answered. "You're welcome to look around."

He had never been much for music. In New York, his apartment had been silent except when she swept into town; Jonathan didn't have a radio, using instead an alarm clock if he needed to wake early. She bought him a radio with a cassette player and used to bring tapes with her from Hartford, anything new she could find, bluegrass, Indian sitar mixed with slide-guitar, Afro-Arab, music from the country he'd recently been to and probably hadn't listened to there. When she found herself recording for him a mix of Aretha Franklin ballads, her favorites, she knew she was in love.

What made it "Presidential," she supposed as she wandered through the suite looking for a radio, was not only the blue and red coloring, the gold-framed glass-top corner tables, the couches at right angles, and the various maroon vases, but the narrow bookshelves that held biographies and coverless history texts with blue and red spines. In the bedroom, the light had a bluish-gold quality reflecting the carpet. The window overlooking Canal Street was open, the curtain still. She tried to see the suite through Jonathan's eyes; he'd said he found these rooms a little scary, but she interpreted this as meaning that he'd been amused by its vastness. It was after seven o'clock and the humidity hadn't let up. The air outside was almost smoky. The smell of wet sidewalks drifted in. It must have rained again.

Jonathan was tidy and kept his few clothes in a small black traveling bag on the wing-backed chair beside the canopied bed. He obviously had no intention of staying longer than was absolutely necessary. The canopied bed's mattress was so thick, the comforter so puffy, it looked as if you needed a stepping stool to climb on. There was no indentation of his long body on the bed, no indication he had taken a few minutes to lie down, but there was a small gray shoe box sitting near the pillow; other than this box and his tiny bag, which looked abandoned, as if they'd been left behind by someone departing in a hurry, the huge room appeared to have no occupant.

Downstairs, in a much smaller room, she had spread her supplies across every surface, tossing blouses onto the second queen bed, covering the top of the television and the counters with papers and sunglasses, her wallet, snacks she had picked up, orange peanut butter crackers, gum. Her husband commented that within five minutes of arriving at a hotel, their room looked like a tornado had passed through; she needed to make a bit of a mess; it was her way of making a place feel like something closer to a home, lived in. Looking at Jonathan's bag, she was touched by how little he needed. On the far side of the bed was a nightstand with a radio.

She smelled onions cooking.

"Is this what you want done?" he asked when she returned, carrying the radio she'd found. He sounded unsure, sweet, a little shy. "I'm at your command, ready to take instructions."

She put the radio on the counter just behind the cutting board where he was working. She tuned it to some zydeco music, a quiet dance number, and picked up another knife. The only sound for a few minutes was blade on wood until she realized they had unconsciously leaned into one another, sharing the board. She was surprised how natural it seemed.

"It sounded from your talk as if you still enjoyed the road," she said. "Tell me all the exotic places you've been. I've barely left my house in the past ten years, you know. I've been extremely unadventurous."

"You had other things to do," he said quietly. "Maybe you're getting to that point in your life again where traveling is possible." Then he remembered she'd said she had a child. He thought about that as he crossed the room to the kitchen table, sat, and stretched out his legs. "You've heard my adventures. Tell me more about your life in the years since. . . ." He looked down at his hands on the counter.

She told him about traveling to Peru soon after Cynthia died (she had to get away), wondering if she would run into him at an airport, afraid to run into him and having to explain herself. She worked at a tiny school in a mountain village where they laid out coffee beans to dry on blankets during the day, and where she could clear her head, alone in her simple room in the cool nights. She told him about how she had gotten married within a year of returning. She told him about her move, six months before, to Portland, Maine, and to a new neighborhood where she still didn't really know anyone. She told him about her father's recent death, and her mother's passing away the year before.

The way Jonathan asked questions—about things that would have been easy to overlook—and listened to her answers, with his head tipped a little to the side, with soft murmurs of agreement, with nearly unnoticeable requests for her to go deeper into what she was saying, was exactly the way she thought she would be listened to by him. When she was younger, she felt that he wanted to know everything about her, but she was sometimes afraid to tell too much. She was afraid he would know her too well, that he would find some weakness in her, some element that would turn him away, maybe even a quality she didn't even realize she possessed. She'd often been angry with him in those days for asking too much of her. Around men, she usually felt confident. Not around Jonathan, though. She understood now that her youthful fears only partly had to do with who he was, that she felt the power of his mind pressing uncomfortably on her sometimes like a hand on her head. Now she knew her own weaknesses; she would be surprised if he found something she didn't already know about herself. Back then, she wanted to keep some secrets from him, and from others. For almost a year, her father didn't know Jonathan existed for her. So little did her father usually ask of her, it seemed like he didn't care. But when he heard about all her time in New York with Jonathan—she remembered telling him during the week before Jonathan left for Nicaragua, it seemed safer then—he couldn't let it go.

"It was never good between you and my father," she said. She put down the knife and sat at the kitchen table.

For a few moments, he kept his back to her. He never should have gone to Nicaragua and he should have come back the day he received her first telegram. Lily had been correct: it was unforgiveable. The day he returned, three weeks after they had buried Cynthia, he remembered calling Windsor, and Lily's father answering.

"It's Jonathan Parrish. I'm so sorry for your loss."

"Okay. What do you want?" He had spoken to Gene Mayeux only a few times that year, and none of them had been welcoming.

"I was hoping to talk to Lily."

"She's not here," he said. "She's out. But I'll give her your message."

When he called back a minute later, her father picked up again.

"Look, she's been treated pretty roughly by you. Enough," Gene Mayeux said.

"I realize you're within your rights not to like me, but I'd appreciate it if you let me talk with Lily."

"You're inconsiderate, but you're not stupid. You'll just have to settle for her *not* talking to you. I'm sure even you can understand why."

Her father picked up the phone every time he called over the next two weeks. Each time Gene Mayeux said only a few words before hanging up. Things like, "Don't bother to drive up here looking for her," or "You can't still be after her. You're not that tasteless, are you?"

He presumed that Mr. Mayeux had never given her his messages. Protecting his daughter, why would he? But Jonathan also presumed that eventually she would call him, ask him what happened. Instead, she had sent a postcard after a few months had passed.

There had been long hours during his drive south yesterday when he cursed himself again for ruining the most important thing of all. He wondered: what kind of man was I? There were hours on the road when he didn't want anything in his head at all; it was too painful. Why hadn't he understood after Cynthia's death—after his absence from her funeral without even sending word—that he couldn't just return home to the way it was? What had he been thinking?

For at least a year, he was humbled by the nature of longing. After another year, he'd gotten used to not seeing Lily. In other countries he was sure of his job; at home, he had less certainty. Audrey, Miriam: the corridors of a woman's heart were never again clear.

He turned to look at Lily. "No. It was never good between me and your father. When I got back from Nicaragua and called, he wouldn't let me speak with you."

She took a deep swallow of beer. It reached her in a clear, strong way. A strange alertness came upon her, and it wasn't a pleasant thing really. Her father had never liked Jonathan. She remembered thinking, in the days after Cynthia's funeral, Jonathan is dead too. That's why he hasn't called. She thought of offering this as an explanation to her father, but she was afraid it was true. Who would let her know for sure, and when? She wasn't related to Jonathan, and she might not hear for weeks if he was hurt or had been murdered in the jungle, she knew. When her father told her, twenty days after the funeral, that Jonathan had called from New York, it had released some force in her. She was relieved that he was alive. But she had already decided to turn away from him. She'd never called him back. For twelve years he had played no part in her private joys.

The zydeco music, dissonant and pained as if crying out someone's name, stilled him. He thought he'd said the things he'd wanted to say. But he wasn't done yet.

"You're right. I still enjoy the travel and the kids. I get to leave a mark behind, even if it's only that an American came and offered some hope in a world where people have been taught to be suspicious of Americans. Even if it's only in getting people to realize they can do more for themselves and their neighbors than they thought they could."

"I don't know if what I'm about to say will mean anything to you. Before we met twelve years ago, I worked and life was interesting and that's all I knew. I loved those countries where no one knew me, and they caught rain in barrels, and the nights were so quiet you could hear motorbikes two miles away. I loved the children I got to work with."

He saw that Lily had closed her eyes. When he was away, it felt truly good to be totally alone, but it felt better having Lily here. The radio, the ceiling fan, the kitchen noises. He'd never been calmer than he was right then.

"For many years, work was all there was in my life. When you came along, I didn't know how to let any part of that life go. There were questions I didn't even want to let in, like where I would live in a year. I was afraid if I stayed still for too long, I'd grow dull in some way."

Her eyes filled with tears and this surprised her. She wanted to remember when everything between them had been good. The beer helped. When was the last time she had actually finished a beer? She remembered some evenings in Hartford when he was out of the country and she would replay old messages Jonathan had left on her phone machine (the machine archived them for ten days, she recalled), not to hear what he said, but only to hear his voice. In those days, she had his quick steps in clogs in her mind like a catchy tune.

She felt like she'd been hiding for twelve years and had just been chased out into the open.

"My father told me each time you called." She was astonished to find herself admitting this to Jonathan. "I was glad you were alive, but I didn't want to speak with you. Not during the weeks you called and not for a long time after."

She felt like an adult and a young woman simultaneously. She was glad to have told him the truth. Her shame, rushing back, was a relief. She had decided, when she found his phone message in her hotel room the day before, that she would try to keep this visit with Jonathan simple, unemotional. But a sweet familiarity had descended over the afternoon and evening. She should never have offered to meet with him. She could hear her breath coming fast. She tried to slow down inside.

He had blamed her father all these years; he was surprised to hear this new version. *She* hadn't taken his calls; *she* had asked her father to intercede. But he knew Lily had been right to walk away of her own free will. His mistake had led them here; there was no taking it back. He sipped his beer and looked down, respectful.

"Let's get some food on the table," she said. They split up the cooking tasks, getting the meal done together. He told her about his recent trip to India, the ornate colored-powder drawings that adorned the walls of people's houses and temples. He told her about the dances he'd seen, the rings of linked arms and twirlings and headstands and men doing splits, the ankle bells and red and yellow paints smeared on their bodies, the drumming and fans and copper pipes that were blown and banged.

As they ate, sitting across from one another at the small white table, his talk of travel seemed like a marvelous dream. It was not what she ever thought about, but now that he had reintroduced it, she thought hard. For the past five years motherhood had claimed her fully. She remembered the last line of his speech: "It's not enough that you move through the world—you must change it to suit your expectations."

"Tell me about your son," Jonathan said. She suddenly wanted to tell him everything: what happened with her, what happened between Jonathan and her, what was supposed to happen. Everything that was in her head at that moment and during the past twelve years.

"Ben is four years old," she said. She thought of tucking her boy into bed, on her knees, her cheek next to his on the pillow, their faces close together.

"My husband's not used to being alone with him for more than a few hours. It will be interesting to see how they fare." She felt guilty mentioning her husband, and could not bring herself to say his name. She liked simplicity and clarity in her life and things felt unclear sitting next to Jonathan Parrish; or rather, she was touched by how clear he was to her after all these years.

Jonathan had always had a sense of her moods. Maybe he would sense her sudden discomfort and finish eating quickly, suggesting that he had some work to do so she could back to her room without being rude.

"Why only one?" he asked.

"One?" Did he mean one beer? One dinner together?

"One child."

She knew she must not speak. It was not necessary to speak, only to remain still a little longer. That was a comfort.

Bluegrass came on the radio. Jonathan Parrish seemed kinder and calmer and more available than she remembered. He was different from the man she'd known.

"My talk tomorrow," she said, changing the subject, trying to lift her mood. "Will you be there?"

"Of course. I'm looking forward to it."

"It will be excellent," she said.

LILY

She let herself into her room and felt immediately, oddly better. Upstairs, she had not been herself, she had not been a nearly middle-aged teacher-mother with a stable marriage and a young son and a husband who couldn't imagine her having lunch and a walk and dinner with the man she'd loved years earlier. Jonathan had asked about Ben and all at once she was in a state of helpless confusion and could not understand any longer what was once obvious to her—why she taught high school, why she lived where she lived, who she shared her life with. She was a wild twenty-two-year-old, ready to charm a man, a little false, a little afraid, not the good listener she thought herself to be, quick to judge. She had gently bragged about tomorrow's talk to Jonathan in part because she felt the need to keep up with his professional success just then, partly because he made her feel proud of herself, partly because she knew he admired her in ways other than her work. She had always been a bit brazen with him. There had been too much to think about in the Presidential Suite. She'd felt on the verge of catastrophe.

When she was twenty-two, she felt anything could happen. And it did with Jonathan, that intoxicating combination of lust and feeling understood. A July day in his New York kitchen, coming up behind him, her bare breasts pressed into his back, her arms around his chest: he smelled like a summer tomato, fragrant, juicy. Standing next to him in a New Orleans hotel suite kitchen, she still had that scent, and when she remembered it she had a moment of dislocation. Seeing him, hearing him talk about his work, she was immersed in his world again. He accidentally brushed her arm and she felt it all the way down to her toes. What biological process she'd taught to ninth-graders ever explained that?

She gazed at the earrings she'd taken off, two drops of malachite. She made a pattern of them, rolling them across her palm before putting them down on the nightstand. She wondered if Jonathan still had trouble sleeping. When she knew him, he stayed up late, almost afraid to try to rest. He had always been a restless sleeper, kicking against her. Often he got up in the middle of the night and quietly slipped away, thinking he hadn't woken her. But she would watch him go to the window and part the curtains and peer out, or tiptoe into the next room and watch television, returning in an hour or two. He never answered his telephone until 10 PM and did all his phoning to his brothers after midnight; he kept the hours of a college student and she understood that if she wanted to reach him, later was better.

Kicking off her shoes and sitting on the edge of her bed, she laughed to herself: of course in New Orleans, a city where the dead were buried above ground. Wasn't that a metaphor for their meeting? New Orleans, the city with the highest murder rate in the nation; perfect too. Your old life gone in a second. From Jonathan she had learned to enjoy the dangers of cities, and the two types of people who lived there, as he put it: those who took what they wanted and those who took whatever they got. New Orleans, a city that smelled tart from the lemon magnolias planted a century before to hide the stench of yellow fever. The French Quarter felt far away from everything, and passionate: the heat, the peppery food, the curling wrought iron of the balconies where molded ferns hung in hemispheric wire baskets.

She lay back, reaching over her head to pull a pillow beneath her neck. She'd never really liked hotel rooms (another reason to avoid these conferences), but she had a lifelong inconsistency in regard to solitude. She liked silence but she didn't like it. She complained about trying to do her homework when Clare sang in the shower; she was driven crazy, when she was on the phone, by Cynthia practicing her flute; her father ran the lawnmower at the worst times; but when the Windsor house was silent she felt lonely and would put on music. Every time she was alone in a hotel room, at some point she imagined that she was the only one in the building, and suddenly terrified, she had to reach for the radio.

Sometimes at these meetings she felt like she was impersonating someone, a mature, striving woman who loved her work. But when Jonathan Parrish talked about traveling it fed some conception of herself that often felt out of reach these days and now seemed concentrated, right. Images drifted through her mind: the strange box on his neat canopied bed; his tempting hands dicing onions, peeling ginger. Needing to avoid his eyes as the meal went on, she foolishly absorbed herself in her beer and in playing with her watch. She felt too present and would have preferred to disappear a bit. As a teacher she disappeared; that was her function. Teachers never spoke of themselves, but focused on their students, and she had grown to prefer this position in the world. She had listed in her mind the characteristics of her classroom self. To teach science was to be unsentimental, to refuse undisciplined responses, to be carefully sympathetic in setting high expectations for her young naturalists. "Do you need to be somewhere?" he'd asked politely when he saw her drifting. When she didn't answer, he'd asked about Ben. This smart, kind, interesting man, this plenary speaker, this superlative man, what did he see in her? Why had he wanted dinner too?

In Maine, she had not yet put down roots in the community of Portland. In Indiana, where Peter had moved them three years before to be near one of his troubled factories, she'd known her neighbors, knew their kids, had a job in an inner-city school where she felt needed, where she could practice the Spanish she had perfected in Mexico as a student with the families from Central America who also found their way to Indianapolis. After six months in Portland—where she had moved again because he'd asked, another factory failing—she still didn't really know her neighbors and they seemed the kind she would never know. At Audubon High School, she was not particularly welcome as the new biology and earth science teacher. People always remarked about the quality of life in coastal Maine, the beauty of the harbors, but she had grown to enjoy the ease of Indiana, the simple greetings on the street.

For all her colleagues' talk, after his speech, of Jonathan Parrish's wild pursuit of his craft, she felt he actually left a quiet footprint. On stage, he emitted tremendous humility. In one way he hadn't changed, she knew after half a day with him: he had a special quality of attention. It made her self-conscious, embarrassed her. Did she really deserve Jonathan's full attention? His listening to her made her want to do her best, to surprise him. He insisted on a version of her that was funny, strange, honest, profound, although this still left her with a tiny hint of envy that he possessed such certainty about her, and that he knew so confidently how to live. She wished she'd brought one of those

Delta beers back to her room; alcohol always inspired a certain optimism.

"We never got to that alligator you brought," she'd mentioned as she was leaving his suite. What a silly thing to have said, but his room had been confusing. It had that hotel unlived-in feel, everything color-coordinated and right-angled, as if orderliness were a style; in a strange way it reminded her of her parents' house in Windsor. Militantly organized by her mother, their living room felt more like a furniture showroom than a home. But the Presidential Suite was also disorienting because she saw the prints of his bare wet feet still sogging the carpet from the bathroom to the chair next to his bed, and this tracing of his steps had moved her in a breathlessly sexual way. She worked then to recall her Portland home, the Mission-style rocker she'd picked out at an antiques store a few months back, the Chinese drawings of mountains Clare had sent her from London.

Seeing Jonathan, she realized she had miscalculated. She had come to New Orleans expecting to escape unscathed, but now she was shaky.

What she wanted—to be able to think clearly about tomorrow's presentation—did not seem possible. Why had she agreed to meet him at all? She moved to the window and parted the filmy white curtains to look down on the still crowded streets of the Quarter, tilting the bottom panel of the window open to let in some street noise. She had always wanted to do significant work, undeniably good work, the quality of which was apparent even to those who taught other disciplines. She tugged at the nearly unmoveable inner curtains, trying to close them a bit to keep out tomorrow morning's light. She took from her suitcase her typed notes. After two minutes, she arrived at the conclusion that her talk was ready, that she was extraordinarily well-prepared. She was tired; she kept reading the same words over and over. She knew Jonathan was leaving the next day, but she hoped it wasn't too early. She wanted him to hear her presentation; she wanted to show off, show him what had become of her.

She should call her husband to say good night, she thought. The week before, on April Fool's Eve, she and Peter and Ben had gone to see the town's fireworks, a chilly Portland tradition. It had been a misty night and she had been surprised that the coordinators had gone ahead with the show. After putting Ben to bed, for the first time in weeks, she and Peter had made love. It had been like the fireworks: the main bright explosions were definitely there and pretty, but much of the detail of the swirly little sparks and smaller pops and fizzes were lost in a blur.

She showered. Walking around the room naked in the warm Southern air felt lovely. She remembered that Jonathan had written her wonderful letters. She wished she had kept them. She'd thrown them all away a month before the wedding. Exhaustive travelogues, details about the food and fashion from wherever he was that week, the hair of the women, the men's footwear. He didn't travel with a camera (although he kept one in his apartment), and didn't believe in pictures he couldn't describe, he claimed. When he got back from an assignment, the first shower always ran off him in an ashen stream, as if one were washing an animal. Jonathan had taught her the pleasures of taking a shower with your lover. She had never taken a shower with a man before him. She was thrilled when he washed her hair. When he held her hard against the wet walls with his chest, his mouth on her mouth, she lost the definition of her body and moved to his touch. She liked long showers to this day because of him. Peter grew cold easily and although she'd invited him over the years, he never really liked sharing the water.

She examined herself in the floor-to-ceiling mirror of the sliding closet door. Although she instinctively frowned, after a moment she liked the look of her reflection. Her eyes first moved to the skin between her breasts, one-third of the way down her sternum, the tiny area where you could first see women aging, even before it showed up around their eyes or on their necks, the patch of chest that became granular and tissuey. Hers was still firm and full. Her breasts had lost little of their shape. In the harsh light, she allowed the question to surface finally: How often had she wondered what would have happened if she'd remained with Jonathan? Not often, but regularly over the years. It was impossible not to have imagined that rejected future, a life of many countries, of vast and enduring adventure, of tiny rooms and rental houses. It was the sense of missed opportunity that returned to her, frightening but real, overwhelmingly real. She touched her lower belly and remembered Jonathan's appendectomy scar like an eraser scratch just over his right hip.

She had wanted to answer Jonathan, tell him why Ben was an only child, but it would have been difficult to begin, and in her desire to talk there would have been the danger of sounding bitter. She wouldn't want him to concentrate on the disappointments in her life. She wanted to explain how, a few days after the second miscarriage three years before, Peter had said, "It wasn't meant to be," said it dispassionately, almost insistently, as if they'd discussed trying again long and thoughtfully and arrived at a conclusion together. In this matter, Peter was so wrong it alarmed her.

Shortly thereafter, they had moved to Indiana. Her husband was happy with Ben, but exhausted by the day-to-day demands of family life and growing problems at work. To avoid the inevitable disagreement and the sense that she was asking for too much, she focused on Ben's adjustment to the new nanny, giving up on the possibility of more children.

She had wanted to stay, to spend three more hours in the Presidential Suite telling Jonathan all about her work, about the boys in her class who smelled of soap and mints, about the girls with their pointed boots and their hair clips attached to a belt loop, more about Ben. She'd also wanted to leave, to prevent that feeling of being overwhelmed which had reappeared. She didn't know what he was thinking. She met his eyes and saw something she couldn't quite recognize. Was he suffering? Was it hope? Of course she couldn't read his expressions confidently and she was surprised that she couldn't; not surprised, saddened. She realized that she didn't really know him anymore.

When she came out of the shower, the light on her phone was blinking red again. "Thank you for dinner. I was very moved hearing a little about Ben."

She called him back, planning to hang up if he answered, preferring to leave a message. "Would you have breakfast with me at 8? This time you can help me with my talk."

JONATHAN

When Lily closed the door, he turned back toward the kitchen, took a deep breath, and let it out very slowly. His world began to slip back into place. The visit with her had caught him unprepared and left him tired, he presumed from disappointment. He didn't want to be alone; the feeling was new and very real. Being alone had always been simplest for him, but it wasn't enough. He didn't have to go back to being simple.

Lily, ravishing Lily. The hungry-hearted watchful aura he had always responded to in her, that he was keen to connect to, that made him know he wasn't out there alone, that he'd felt during his speech although he couldn't see her, was still present. She had left to make sure he didn't get the wrong idea.

He wondered how her bare shoulders would feel after all these years, her back's strong muscles, how her hips would fit in his palms, and how, holding fast, her pelvis would look, down the length of his body, going high and descending. He tried to think of other things, the route he would take home, what time he would leave the next day, whether he would swing east or west as he headed toward New England. Then he pictured the way she threw back her head when she laughed, and the red hair between her legs.

Back then, each weekend that she visited New York seemed new and distinct, he recalled, and today had been just as dizzying. At the kitchen sink, he ran cold water over his face. He struggled to put her out of his mind just as he had during those first moments in the darkness years before when they left the house with open Ball jars in search of fireflies. He tried to think of the rules that should constrain him now, the years apart, the decade of propriety. But he failed and wondered again about the flex of her neck, its shadowy pulse, whether he could recall the exact size of the faded birthmark near her knee. All the old feelings fighting toward the surface.

She still exuded an aspect of invincibility and intelligence which he remembered from before. Perfect for a teacher of teenagers, and no one appreciated this more than he. Even at twenty-two she knew more about what she wanted than he did, he believed. She was aware of her own impatience; she asked him not to leave the country again, warned him not to, teasingly he thought. It was his fault. He had been foolish in leaving, work had taken over. What did he expect? It was somehow better that she was still married. It signaled loyalty, and that she hadn't fully lost her senses after his disappearance or in the years after.

He was seized by her tales of Windsor. It wasn't only the secret history of Lily Mayeux she was revealing, or even of the Mayeux clan; it was the secret history of his own youth, of his old house and its sights and smells, of his brothers and parents. It was his childhood, his younger life, his lifeline to love. She knew his history, but seen from outside. And Lily was not just the keeper and narrator of this intimate knowledge but a participant; she was memory incarnate, sentiment incarnate, and this intensified and complicated his hunger for her way beyond lust, which was painful enough, into something different and blind. He had wanted to be quiet with her at dinner so that he could listen to her. Lust and mourning for the past slid by and he'd said things that he hoped hadn't sounded false. He wanted to hear the story of why she married someone else, in order to relieve the pressure of all his imaginings about what happened. He was ready to experience that sense of loss that had torn him apart because he trusted she would tell it truthfully now, with this distance, and he didn't mind getting a little bloody. But she hadn't told him and now he wasn't certain that she would if he didn't ask, and asking seemed like intruding even though it was his story too.

Before he set out for New Orleans, if he'd been honest with himself, he would have been aware of the complications that might develop in his emotions when he arrived. Twelve years before he had misjudged too upon another arrival.

He sensed that he'd found her at a time of transition. The way she spoke of her move to Maine made it clear that she hadn't found her place there yet, that she missed old friends and hadn't seen a way to find replacements, that her work was unsettled. Yet she gave no sign that her marriage was other than stable and affectionate. She had the responsibilities and commitments of the mother of a young child.

He realized that in their hours together he hadn't said her name aloud, nor she his. He used to whisper *Lily* over and over in her ear and she had liked the sound of it coming out of his mouth.

The thought passed through his head that Lily Mayeux was the only woman he had ever really loved.

PART 4: SATURDAY MORNING

LILY AND JONATHAN

She woke thinking of Jonathan, as if he were the singular, obvious subject of her day. It was strange, another strange thing in this strange situation, Lily thought. It seemed like some steps had been skipped, or else that no time had passed in all this time. It reminded her of knitting. Several times she had put down something she was working on in the middle of a row, ended up storing it away, then picked it up years later, looked it over to see where she was, then gone ahead with the next stitch.

What can ever equal the memory of being young together? This was his first morning thought under the golden canopy of his bed. He had loved Lily at his most optimistic moment. He remembered the taste of her tongue, its shy slipperiness. Could he ever forget that?

She was stunned with how comfortable she was with him. Did they really know each other? How could they after all these years? Yet there was some sort of understanding. Some force flowed between them. He *did* know her. She could feel it on her skin. She was tongue-tied; it was too large for language.

A quick look in the mirror before he went downstairs for breakfast. He ran his fingers through his hair, smoothed the front of his shirt; that was the best he could do. He thought of stopping at the stand outside the hotel to buy her more flowers, but it felt like too much. He had brought the flowers to lunch the day before as a peace offering. He brought them because he grew sunflowers in the summer and thought they were beautiful, and he wanted her to know that he loved beautiful things. He brought them because they would remain with her when he was gone, and they would remind her. He brought them to see if she had changed, if she still warmed to flowers as she had in her unsentimental, skeptical youth. He brought them to savor the pleasure of watching her receive them. He brought them because he wanted to give her something, and not arrive empty-handed, which was to say, Expect nothing from me.

She permitted herself another minute in bed. Once she saw him, anything could happen. She was calm, although her mind hummed. It felt like a good day. She glanced at the clock. The frenetic pace of the meeting made her feel idle. She'd never gotten enough done in her career; she never would. Going downstairs to the conference room for this morning's featured speeches before her smaller talk at 11 AM, her sideshow, would depress her, she decided. When she went to make coffee (they always placed the coffeemaker unappetizingly near the bathroom), she did not look directly into the mirror. She was aware of her reflected movement (both sliding doors of the closet were mirrors), but she did not glance up. She walked over to the sunflowers and inhaled deeply. They had a mild scent. They were very beautiful: stiff yellow shrines. She decided not to meet him for breakfast.

When she hadn't appeared at the restaurant where they'd had lunch by 8:00, he called his room to check for messages. Had he heard her incorrectly the night before? Had she left a note at the hotel's front desk? Nothing. Perhaps she just wanted to rework her talk alone, without his interference, and she needed time. When he found no new message from her, he called her room. No answer. She hadn't taken his calls years ago, and he remembered his younger brother phoning him to ask why Lily had returned the keys to his New York apartment; Paul had never forgiven her in all these years. Jonathan had no doubt the same thing was happening this morning: she was receding into the life she had. With characteristic self-discipline, she had stopped this before it went too far; it was the same discipline that got her married and kept her married, an instinct not to jeopardize the future. His mistake had been to fall under the spell of his work so completely as to not rush to Lily when she needed him. Of course she was angry. She suspected him of the worst kind of cruelty, he supposed, and her grievance was justified.

He should have known she would do this last night, when the decades hovered over the dishes. Too many things stood between them. A hotel was not conducive to romance, to persuasion, to reunion. He was ready to scribble out a note in protest, but he knew his words would not affect her decisions. There'd been a difference in Lily at dinner that hadn't seemed great at the time, but seemed great now. Of course she was gone, a married woman.

She refused to give herself over to another meal of shared secrets. At dinner, sitting next to him, she had felt herself grow wet between the legs and it was too much. Something about it felt like surrender, like she was relinquishing. She felt like she had to turn away. Back then, she was angry that he'd left. But in retrospect, she realized that twenty-three-year-old Lily Mayeux must have had a sense that she didn't deserve Jonathan Parrish. Twenty-three-year-old Lily knew as clearly as anything that it was her fault he'd left; she'd driven him away, or he would have changed his plans and passed on going to Nicaragua that last time; it had been his choice, she remembered. She'd been an idiot that spring, asking him to stay. Jonathan had never been able to stop himself from wandering; he had no choice, she now realized. His excuses and explanations seemed elaborate in hindsight. She had cried easily in the days before he flew off, palming her face. She hadn't cried once in his view, though; she'd acted bravely. And after he left her, she left him. Was it retaliation for choosing work over her? It wasn't something she'd decided before he left. But then Cynthia died. Her father got involved, which she knew was not easy for him. Her friends had seen her stoicism. She didn't really care what anyone thought; not when she decided to be with Jonathan, not when she decided to no longer see him. Privately, she bore the guilt of betrayal which was stirred up over the years whenever she had to go to New York, or by the aroma of certain spices. She hadn't eaten Indian food in twelve years.

He accepted the proposition that to follow what obsessed and excited him and was viscerally, though often mysteriously, part of his life was to live "better," to live with more conviction and energy. But, he had learned, it was also arduous and sometimes disappointing.

That all of this could open again so fast disturbed Lily. She had mustered all her rationality the night before, all her moral discipline to behave as a devoted wife. But then again, Jonathan hadn't suggested anything directly. She was, at dinner, unsettled, confused. Why was he so kind, so undemanding? Did he really accept her as the person she was now? Had they silently agreed to the limits of friendship? He'd seen her last as a naïve young woman, but she had come to New Orleans with a life behind her, a difficult life she was proud of. She felt that he saw her outside time, as the person he'd always known. She could handle this today only by avoiding him or by displaying her desire. She had thoughtlessly suggested breakfast. She blamed herself for poor judgment. Until she saw Jonathan yesterday, she took no pleasure in looking back, and seldom did. Her youth felt like a remote period, a period forsaken and mournful, dimly visible, a time when she'd felt weak.

He could feel on his skin the return of humiliation from twelve years before. He understood that after she'd announced she would not to see him again, no one in her family would have defended him. He understood why. He was dangerous, a stray dog, thin, perhaps pathetic, hungry, never to be tamed. Together for almost a year, they had bewildered people.

He went out into the French Quarter to find a place to eat breakfast. The Quarter was nearly empty. The streets had a tranquility he didn't associate with New Orleans. Before 9 AM many cafes were closed. He could hear televisions or radios on behind the closed shutters of apartments. The curbs smelled of alcohol, as if they had been washed down with bourbon, but the garbage from the previous night's revelry had been picked up and he spotted only a few half-filled plastic cups still lodged on window-sills. It was already steamy. Residents were out walking dogs and he saw an older woman with a Cairn terrier. Lily always stopped to pet Cairns in particular. There were other things she liked: grass that grew between cobblestones, white churches with red doors. Disappointed that he was alone, he tried to distract himself. He had always enjoyed disappearing into the market streets of a new tropical city, and New Orleans felt Caribbean—the cats, the wet gutters, the louvered windows, the sky no longer a circle, but like decking, divided into planks. His favorite kind of morning, a walk with no particular destination. He began to appreciate the heat of the day and its swelling humidity. Maybe he should have left well enough alone with Lily; one dinner was enough. Then he thought: at the last moment maybe something had made her avoid coming this morning and he wondered if she had fallen ill or received bad news from home. At a coffee shop, he stopped for a croissant and to use the pay phone.

When the phone in her room rang and she didn't pick it up, she could imagine Jonathan cursing himself. She felt cruel and embarrassed. Instead of answering, she wrote a note she would ask the concierge to have delivered to his room. "Please excuse me for not joining you for breakfast. I had to prepare my talk."

Twice, once before and once after he'd eaten breakfast, he saw a woman come toward him from a distance that blurred her features. Both times he prepared himself to recognize Lily and to be recognized, but it was not her.

When he got back to the hotel he found two messages from her at the front desk. The first one read, "Please excuse me for not joining you for breakfast. I had to prepare my talk." He knew what she'd written was nonsense. The second one: "I was scared of you then and I still am." He read on. "How about dinner tonight?"

It was not that she had revised her feelings. It felt like their old love story and this new one were coming together, joining, mingling. Since arriving in New Orleans, she couldn't shake the dual sense of both being where she was and having drifted back to a time she could still sense palpably on her flesh, a time that laid bare a young and innocent idea of life. She experienced history as a force.

She knew there was some risk in seeing him again for dinner, but she felt compelled. Jonathan had changed. After she wrote the first note, suddenly everything was obvious and she wrote the second one. She wasn't ready to give him up again so quickly this time.

On the raised dais in a smaller conference room than the one Jonathan had spoken in the day before, she sat behind a table with the other panelists. She noticed him along the wall, trying to hide. It was almost entertaining to watch him. He stood out in this crowd. Tall and graceful, and wearing a black T-shirt, not dressed like anyone else. She could see his forearms whose length and shape had always appealed to her, crossing and uncrossing in indecision, the muscles tight. He didn't hurry to find a seat. She could see his loose body trying to decide whether to slip into one of the middle rows where he would be trapped for several talks, or to stay along the sidelines where he might be spotted by her and seem intrusive after she'd avoided him at breakfast. He had placed himself at a respectful distance. She watched him squat, his back flat against the wall for support—the only one in the aisle, the only one squatting—anticipating whether he would be able to see her face from that lowered angle. An angle where he might remain unseen. She was happy, strangely happy, watching him struggle with this tiny decision. It made her smile to think he was contorting himself for her sake. She felt surprisingly calm—more relaxed than usual for such an occasion.

The wall was actually a mobile partition and when he rubbed against its nubbly, tan, almost carpeted, soundproofed texture, it gave a little bit, shifted with him. He could faintly hear the lecture in the next room through it. He scanned the room, the rows of seats, rows of legs, one hauled across the other, fish-white skin appearing at the ankles. He wanted to remain out of her line of vision. What was he doing, inching around a conference room? He felt himself grin in mild embarrassment. In the semi-darkness, she probably couldn't see him even if she knew he was there.

When she approached the tiny light of the lectern, he appreciated, not for the first time, that she was unlike the other teachers at this meeting. Her posture was perfect and she knew something about style. She dressed carefully for her talk, a tailored blazer and a gray silk skirt. Gold rings dangled from her ears. And a single strand of jade beads. She didn't look like a teacher from a public school in Maine. Where had she gotten such poise and presence? Breakfast; he wouldn't have been able to eat much anyway.

At twenty-three, she had never spent much time in personal analysis. She trusted the validity of her emotions and accepted her initial reactions to people without question. He had prized this quality in her—it was brave to be with a man eight years her senior—but now, he realized, it made his case hopeless. His case? What was he thinking? He was proud of her, he admired her, and at that moment he was conscious of life as something good and he fell in love with her all over again. This consciousness of love took the form of a deep patience inhabiting him, rather than a feeling of cheer or even hope.

She wore something for his sake, something that he would notice and consider beautiful, jade beads that she wore rarely at home. She had packed them when she read his name in the program.

Jonathan's great gift to her at twenty-three was confirming her freedom from fear. Looking out across her audience, she remembered this just before she began to speak. Despite the decorum of the occasion, she was aware of herself, her force, when she set her papers down. She had promised him an excellent talk in her session on "Difficult Classrooms."

Troy Gleason was a boy she found fascinating, frightening, and endearing. Troy was tall for a ninth grader with groups of pimples around his sideburns and along his upper lips, those areas where he had just begun to shave. He carried a diagnosis of Disruptive Impulse Disorder, which he himself warned her about the first day of class. "I'm better now," he said. "The medications are helping." He always spoke in a loud voice.

The disorder came on when he had to speak publicly. He would start rubbing his temple with his palm. And when he opened his mouth, he couldn't get started in presenting what was on his mind. It was like a stutter, but he didn't get caught on letters—s's or t's or g's—but on phrases: "So, so, so I decided to, and there was, and there was and there was music on, so I had this idea, it was crazy, it was crazy. . . ." When he knew he was losing control, he would shake his head, his voice growing louder. "I don't know what I'm saying. Forget it. Forget it. Forget it." He would start to fade into a self-deprecating mumble then his body would start to shake, and he would yell out, "Oh fuck it. Never mind." The other children would be shocked, scared, shifting uncomfortably in the presence of a classmate who was clearly a maniac and a threat. It was terrifying to watch, the frustration and lack of inhibition.

But Lily explained how Troy could be talked back from the brink of explosion. How he was extremely bright—he had quite a three-dimensional sense and excelled at anatomy—and was eloquent when he managed to get going. How Troy's honesty about his condition allowed her to exhibit a patience she hadn't known she harbored. She explained her strategy of allowing him to get up and pace before he had to speak, to release some of the pressure that built inside of him, and how other children thought she favored Troy and gave him special consideration. She described how it was possible to lead a classroom filled with disruptions, that disruptions in life presented an opportunity for everyone to slow down and reconsider.

"How many legs are there in the room?" his father would ask Lily when she came for a visit. "Take a guess. Quickly. No counting."

"How many what?" she asked the first time she was tested, the first time she came to the Parrish house as Jonathan's lover.

"Legs. Chairs, humans, tables."

This is what he remembered when he considered her view from the podium as the applause rose and she smiled from behind the lectern. Was she counting the legs in front of her, multiplying length by width across this auditorium of fold-up chairs, and multiplying again by four? He could hear his father's voice. He could imagine his parents' living room with its framed replica of the Constitution and the bronze Abraham Lincoln bust on the mantle which demanded a certain respect, in contrast to the teasing older man in the bridge chair. Lily had enjoyed his father's imposing good looks and easygoing diplomacy.

As he settled against the partition, he could see Lily Mayeux coming into the house in her woolen ski hat, childlike, still tomboyish at twenty-two. After that first time, she'd put on her face of furious combat and start calculating as soon as she stepped inside the front door, before his father could say, "Time's up. What your number?"

When he approached her after the talk and she saw him staring at her neck, at the jade beads, she began to blush. She knew she was blushing because her body was on fire. Was her body on fire because he was granting her such attention? Because she had guessed what he liked? Because he knew she was wearing the beads for his sake? No. It was because her desire was so violent she couldn't contain it. He didn't look like those he stood among with their bellies and comfortable, soft shoes. He was tall and sharpened. She could see the muscles of his shoulders through the light cotton shirt. Within her body she sensed a powerful, ferocious, expanding wave of heat.

It was the Southern humidity that made her flush, he supposed, the wave of heat that entered the meeting room when they opened the rear doors at the end of the session. Or the result of the fiery answers she had given to questioners who, at the completion of her talk, had lined up at microphones in the aisles to offer their doubts about her message of patience. He could see sweat on her upper lip. Maybe her red face showed the bodily sensation of having escaped a huge peril, which was what he often felt after he had spoken in public. Then another idea, completely opposite, caught him by surprise: his unexpected appearance in this auditorium had caused her to blush from the shame of standing him up at breakfast. When he came nearer, he saw her face brighten with a secret amusement. He did not want to ask why she was smiling.

What she hadn't said in her talk, which didn't fit in a lecture to this audience, but which she knew to be true, was that a good teacher could discern a child's inner turmoil in a face or even from the movements of a body. Without a word, without asking a question, a teacher could know not only a child's immediate and past classroom problems, but his history of tragedy, resistance, pride, nonchalance, restraint. She could know the demands on a student's psyche, his self-criticisms, his wounds.

"Come by at seven," he said when the other questioners had drifted away. "This time I'll cook."

LILY

After his offer to cook, she told him that she had to hurry to the session of a friend. She liked to be occupied, usually keeping herself busy at these meetings. The number of people one knew at conferences was a product of age and professional advancement. Instead, she rode up in the glass elevator at the northern end of the enormous atrium, while across a mirror elevator dropped, as if they were two weights on opposite ends of a scale. She stepped out of the elevator on the twelfth floor into a corridor that was missing half a wall, that was open on her right to the currents of atrium air rising from the lobby. She stayed away from this half-wall; its view made her vertiginous. Hugging the inner wall, she started toward an unattended cleaning cart at the end of the hall to ask a maid for an extra towel, but she felt spoiled near maids and wanted to spare them any work. After opening her door with the swipe of a card, she reached inside, lifted the DO NOT DISTURB sign, and hung it on the outside knob. She stepped inside her room. Safe. She moved past the bed and opened the heavy, greasy curtains. She needed some air. Turning away from the window, her eyes stopped on the sunflowers in the water glass she'd set beside the telephone. She thought past lunch when there would still be whole hours of afternoon left. There was no room for idleness at a conference like this one. At least not for the teachers downstairs meeting and meeting. There was no room for idleness because there were so many lives to be saved, so many students to be helped, tricks of the trade to be exchanged in each room. The teachers downstairs forced themselves toward encouraging talk.

At conferences, she seemed to pick up speed. But today, like Jonathan, who seemed unhurried in all his movements, she wanted to allow herself a lapse. Too many obligations; did this need to be another one, participation? She wanted to knit, to relax.

Very bulky yarn was fun because it knit up so fast, but for physical enjoyment, she preferred a nicely proportioned wool or cotton, like a worsted weight or a little lighter, that didn't easily get split by an off-target needle; nothing too fuzzy, so that the structure of the work was easily visible. When she started to develop her personal knitting style, she planned patterns of knits and purls that would lead to nice effects like the cuff being snug, and the arm being loose, the cable pattern being centered on the chest, and then she worked out the arithmetic so that those patterns would join up to make a whole garment that would fit, be comfortable, and look good. Sometimes working out the arithmetic was hard—a design challenge. She usually didn't use patterns, because she liked to do the work herself, but some were quite inspiring and beautiful just in their design arithmetic. She especially liked seamless sweaters, where the arm tubes and the body tube were grafted together. She really hated patterns where they asked you to make several different flat pieces and sew them together. So inelegant, such a misunderstanding of the potential of knitting.

She called home without a plan for what to say if Peter asked whom she'd seen, whom she'd eaten with. What would she answer? Jonathan has returned, still sweet-smelling, but now sweet-tempered as well? But her husband was unlikely to ask. When Peter picked up, she could hear her husband moving around in the kitchen as they spoke, banging a pan, pouring milk, beating an egg. The bleating of a microwave—oatmeal for Ben, coffee reheating, bacon? At home, she made good coffee, she told herself. She took good care of her husband and child. Her hand on the receiver was trembling, but she was cheerful, loving, trying not to be possessed by the dreamlike feeling that was overtaking her. A loving phone call: that should compensate, shouldn't it?

It had been a sudden, illogical attraction. He was arrogant, provocative, eight years older, ambitious, more than a school teacher even then. Over the years she'd thought about him, his contradictions, what scared her, why her father hated him, her father dead now. Jonathan's intensity, his probing. Her confusion, the possibilities, her sense of something important happening and happening. He returned to her in flashes as short-lived as the views from the train window on the return to Hartford.

She felt young again. The last twenty-four hours had allowed a slow unremitting pull she recognized. A thrill and a comfort. She loved the way Jonathan was put together, the design of his chest, his tight waist, the swiftness of his mind. She had kept secret the exorbitance of her love for Jonathan even when they were together. With friends, out of unwritten laws not to speak of passion (was it really just fear of losing it?), she censored herself in her descriptions of him, the absoluteness of her love. In their years apart she had never really conceived of Jonathan getting older, *couldn't* conceive of it. He had arrived as she remembered him: long-legged, an egret, an exclamation point. She had come to New Orleans with every intention of being cheerful, warm but distant, yet until this moment, she realized, she had been tense, edgy, struggling. She no longer doubted what it meant, the fiery assault on her body that she hadn't been able to control after her speech. She couldn't hide it, cover it. Was she ready?

She tried to have several knitting projects going at once. Ideally, she had one that was at a stage where she didn't need to look (that she could work on while reading), one that had a fancy pattern stitch or color pattern that required some visual attention, but not much thought (for when she was a passenger in a car), and one that was at a stage where she actually needed to think about it (the structure or progression of the pattern, increases, decreases) for the kind of unspoken-for time that she hardly ever had any more. Right then, she was making a striped sweater for Ben from yarn he chose (little thought or attention), and a sweater for herself from hand-dyed wool from Scotland (stalled because she needed the right moment to think about grafting the sleeves and body while incorporating a beetle pattern she had designed for the chest).

JONATHAN

He had the urge to be in his garden on an August day, clearing weeds, spreading mulch. He liked to be out early in the morning, when the ground was still wet, or late in the afternoon, when the air was almost smoky. The water would be running, his hands scented with arugula, tomato. He would peel the slugs off the lettuce, stopping to lift his cup of coffee off the post. An hour a day working his fingers through the soil, listening to the wind bend the pines. He'd heard spring coming in the tops of the trees the morning he left Burlington, the wind with a new ticket into town. Trees set free, in rebellion against winter, screaming, restless, nervous. Trees done with boring bloodless winter. Trees discovering a new language and modeling new thoughts. That's all it took to preserve mental health: the seasons of Vermont changing. He wanted his garden and his cigarette and his trees, and he wanted Lily inside his house waiting.

He was not hungry for the dinner he was about to serve her. There was no food he could present that would be easily digested. He was distracted. He was consumed by fleeting thoughts and fragments of memory that dissipated swiftly. Years before, he had been careless with her in small ways, ways that counted. In his inability to remember something she'd told him, the name of a friend. In not cleaning his apartment adequately before she visited. In his slowness in laughing at jokes she brought him from Hartford. Maybe once in a while, but not often, getting it right.

Just as Lily's decision to be with him when she was twenty-two was rebellious, her decision not to see him again was as well. She had once been prepared to accept a new life and move on. He supposed he was the weaker of them, she the stronger. Why, all these years later, did the far-off past matter anymore? Why should he even take an interest? When he saw her name on his program, it reawakened the obsessions of youth and life with all its possibilities and passions. He understood she was not available, understood the limitations of the situation. He wouldn't misjudge, believing she was under the spell of the moment. He would appreciate the coincidence of this shared two-day conference as a wonderful, fortunate gift.

It was impossible to read her, how she was sizing him up, what she intended. But he had things to say. When she was twenty-two he'd asked her: what is the most foolish thing you've done, the most vile, the most thrilling, the hardest, the most frightening? He wanted to hear an update. But this time, when he needed to say something important to her, he had no words for it.

Her son. When he brought up her son he was letting her know in the surest, strongest way, instantly, fully, that everything of hers was of great interest to him.

PART 5: SATURDAY EVENING

JONATHAN AND LILY

"I'm ready," she said, entering the kitchen. He had left the door ajar and she had let herself in. "For dinner."

Trying to find a way to normal conversation, they spoke quietly about the conference, the cars backfiring on the street outside the hotel as it grew dark. They spoke about places they would each like to travel. He told her he wanted to take a train across Canada. She wanted to see the Amazon Basin and Patagonia. He wanted to drive across the deep American South, Mississippi, Arkansas.

"Maybe I'll go with you if you quit smoking," she said.

"Quit again, you mean." He'd stopped after the first night they spent together in New York, stone cold lost his taste for nicotine.

He spoke with his hands. She was interested in his naked wrists. Had he ever worn a watch? She couldn't remember. What did it say about a man, not owning a watch? Yet he had an uncanny ability to know the correct time. He complained about people who kept him waiting. Sometimes she would miss the early train and show up later than he expected. She remembered defending herself by telling him he ate meals at odd times anyway.

Dinner this evening: gazpacho and cooked artichokes. Between the words and laughter of their conversation, he coughed. She remembered the cough. The sweet embarrassed cough arrived when he was nervous; he was unaware of it.

"Are you hungry?"

"Not very, now that you ask," she answered. She stalled, looking for her balance, losing it.

Delta beer. As if she knew the bottle inside and out, as if she'd seen it her whole life, instead of having her first the day before. The heavy humidity had turned into fat drops of rain which pattered on the sill outside the kitchen and matched the condensation on the glass in her hand.

She was pleased with how she looked. The dress she'd worn was light and stopped at the top of her knee. She was pleased that he noticed her legs. He was attentive to everything. His slightly amused, mock self-important smile, then a more serious version of the smile. He leaned easily against the counter, legs crossed.

His inability to keep his eyes off her had always been a wonderful erotic mystery. What was he doing? Dinner should be quick and he should drive north, get out of town tonight. Get back to your garden and your painting and the professor of anthropology who wants to date you, whom you've slept with from time to time, he told himself. But all he could think about was Lily Mayeux and the old love rode steadily up and over him.

He had not worn a watch since he lost his father's in Bangkok a year earlier, he told her when she asked. A stretchable golden metal band, one that caught the hairs of his forearm. Old-fashioned—not water-resistant, requiring a tiny winding of its serrated edge between thumb and forefinger. Slide a nail under this same disc to pull it away from the body of the machine, engaging a different gear to turn the hands and reset the time. It made a tiny ticking noise he could always hear.

She listened to him quietly, almost as if she were trying to hear its absent ticking. Why was she so quiet? Because she believed if she said nothing time wouldn't go by. It would stop, as if waiting for her next words. With her mouth closed, time came to a standstill. It wasn't that she had nothing to say; rather, she had too much to say. Every simple, ordinary phrase that she hadn't said to him for twelve years.

"Do you still knit?" he asked.

Before she answered, she let the past reveal itself to her. Her mother taught her to knit when she was six. She made a tiny pair of mittens with no thumb—little sacks, really—for a new baby cousin. By the time she finished, the baby had outgrown them. It was frustrating, and it made her hands tired because she held the yarn and pulled the stitches too tight, like most beginners. At the start of college, she took it up seriously. She enjoyed every part of the process except finding knots in the yarn. If there was more than one knot in a skein, she resolved not to buy that brand again. Most of her projects since Ben was born had not presented any particular new challenge, because that wasn't really what she was knitting for now. She did think about some technical demands, strategies for using different weights of wool in the same piece, but mostly she knit for the calming process and useful end product these days. She was looking forward to designing some complex projects later, when Ben was older, but they just didn't fit her life right now. "I do," she said. "Every day. But tell me more about your garden. Do you grow sunflowers?"

How did she know that the sunflowers he'd given her were a way of connecting her to his life in Vermont? There was nothing to fear from this visit; she'd come to lunch yesterday to get a look at him, to see what had become of him. She'd come to dinner to sit at this table and talk a little more before they disappeared from one another again. Dinner tonight? Maybe she was still waiting to hear what happened, to draw the hard-to-fathom out into the open. He remembered the one Thanksgiving they'd spent together at his brother Paul's house in New Canaan and the great, unforeseen gusts of feeling he had sitting across from her when she told the room about the summer work she once had in

the forests of Ontario counting seed pods and measuring specia-
tion with a woman botany professor of hers. In New Canaan, she
had been fifteen miles from her parents' house in Windsor and
hadn't called.

"Worms," he said, "does your son like worms? I have plenty
in my garden."

The possibility of bringing Ben to Vermont to see Jonathan
and his worms was stirring. It was as if he already knew her
son. Hadn't Ben just been on a worm spree? Every evening after
dinner he wanted to go straight to the park to look for them.
Offered a choice, he preferred worms to ice cream (not that
he wanted to eat worms). He knew that the plastic rake was a
better tool than the plastic shovel because worms could often
be found by raking away parts of the heavy blanket of old leaves
that lay around the edge of the playground, the worms hanging
out between the leaves and the dirt. "They like me, they know
I'm careful with them," he would say. He liked the vigorous ones
and would ask if she had any snacks for his worms. "The worm
chips have dirt on the inside, right Mommy, and they have worm
salt on the outside?"

Thinking of her son, she felt strong and direct. She could
speak honestly, tell Jonathan what happened twelve years before
without humiliation. She *needed* to see Jonathan Parrish today
and, she realized, seeing him brought revelations. She felt her
emotions were further along than they should have been, but it
also seemed of the greatest importance to be with him just now.
Was it excitement or fright she was feeling? She had passed right
by skepticism into astonishment. She'd never forgotten how he
looked, but she had forgotten how it affected her.

Listening to her, Jonathan remembered sudden apparitions
that used to spring without warning into his head during their
year together. They were fragments of landscape: the view of a
lake from a dock, a vertical of cragged granite that looked like

bones above the tree line, a golf course at night. They were images of her: Lily reading aloud from the newspaper. Lily touching the sensitive scar under her chin. Lily stretched out along a picnic bench, her toes wriggling. Lily holding an eyelash on her fingertip. She had always haunted him. In dreams, he sometimes saw her undressing; he saw her face, eyes closed. Such dreams woke him. He was an expert at snapping his mind shut when he needed to, but today he was angry with himself for having closed up before he returned from Nicaragua, and having lost her.

She unconsciously touched her jade necklace, raised her fingers to the spot under her chin. Her father had stitched her up in the kitchen. She must have been eight or nine years old. After one or another fight with her sister, she had come in bleeding, cut by the edge of a coffee table she'd fallen over trying to escape Clare's wrath. Her father lay her down on the orange formica counter and tipped her head back into the sink so that the blood from her chin ran down the drain. He always kept a bottle of sterile water in the house, along with his needles and suture thread. On her back, she stared at the stucco ceiling, the swirls and texture, and imagined the arms of the plasterers moving in semi-circles and circles. She thought of the cricks in their necks and drips that must have fallen in their eyes and down their faces like sticky white tears. Her father never said much, maybe he whispered, "Hold still now." He had stitched her before and sometimes he would use a numbing medicine on her skin and sometimes he wouldn't, depending on what he had in the house; she believed the decision was also partly based on whether he was trying to toughen her up that month. She knew he didn't want to drive twenty minutes into town to have someone else do the sewing. She jumped off the counter and ran straight for the mirror to see his work. Stitches were a sign of bravery and she admired the perfectly straight lines he tied with the running black thread.

He hadn't lost her. He had chosen not to go after her when he returned to the United States. He didn't have the strength to pursue her when it was clear that she didn't want to see him. She had never tried reaching him in New York after the funeral. He didn't pursue Lily because he wanted her to love him as much as he loved her and over time he concluded she didn't. At thirty-one, he had been struck by the absurdity of a search—of course he could find her, but why seek a woman who was running from him? She didn't want to be found. He had had then the strange feeling that what was happening was not real, could not be real; the same feeling he had yesterday when she agreed to be found. For years he experienced Lily as a dual character: she was every-where and nowhere. Today, she was here.

Jonathan led her into the living room when she said she wasn't hungry. She had a flash of his old apartment: the tables littered with papers and wine glasses and coffee cups, a room full of unpredictability and unrest. In New York, she could tell he didn't know the right time to kiss her. His almost childish embar-rassment flattered her then, a sign of his bewildered love for her. It was as if he'd invited her to his city under false pretenses at twenty-two. He thought she didn't know what she was getting into, when actually she had thought out everything in advance and she knew perfectly well. She expected and looked forward to making love that first time. She remembered he was confused when he discovered that she knew him so well. He was older now but still slightly awkward.

On the glass table in front of the couch where he invited her to sit was the gray shoebox she'd seen the day before on his bed. She understood even before he opened it: his heartbreak box. For the space of a few seconds, the idea was painful to her. She couldn't have guessed what form his grief had taken over the years. But here it was; she could feel it now. When he lifted the lid, gently as if it were pottery, she saw his secret store of sacred objects. A box of praise, a box of innocence. She accepted the honor of it. The romance of it.

He first picked out the letters she'd written to him from the train back to Hartford after each weekend visit. She saw her twenty-two-year-old writing, sizable, leaning to the left. She still wrote the same way. In what ways had she changed? She was no longer certain.

The photo of her standing naked on his Indonesian kitchen table. It had been kept in the box and so had not faded and she was the young woman she had been. Confidently smiling, the sun defining her red hair like a glamorous dahlia. She had paraded onto his table and he had paid attention with this picture. That was how he saw her and that was how she wanted to remain, full length in the frame, her hand against her hip like the handle of a cup, the tiny grooves around her eyes. She was pleased tonight even though she shook her head.

"And these are the gifts I bought on your birthday each year, although I couldn't give them to you."

A green silk purse. Hand-painted earrings. A tiny birdcage. A thick bronze bracelet worn by hunters.

Her immediate concern was not to cry—from relief, shame, self-pity, she didn't know which was which; all came at her. Her throat tightened. It was impossible to speak.

The postcard. The one she'd written to him after Cynthia died. She lifted it out of the box. The woman sitting at her desk in the middle of an empty loft, the floor strewn with straw or hemp. She turned it over, remembering the words she'd written: "I can't now. But you'll know I wasn't finished with you." She laid it down beside the undelivered gifts.

For the first time since arriving in New Orleans, he saw in her eyes a gleam of complicity. He had seen terrified looks, expressions of frightened astonishment. Each came to this city, he knew, without knowing what to expect from the other. Every certainty could have turned out to be illusory. Years before, when he began to save objects in the box, he was not thinking he would see her again. He had no plan, intended no future. He simply wanted to keep her, to rid himself of the idea that she was gone. The things in themselves were insignificant, but became important over time because they were an inventory of pain. When he packed the box into his truck, he did not try to foresee her reaction. If he had attempted to guess, he would have supposed she would say simply, You haven't forgotten about me.

"Where is the scarf?" Once she understood what he was showing her, she expected to see the gray cashmere scarf she had knit for him. Of course he never liked getting presents. Whenever she used to ask what he wanted, he would tell her not to get him anything. When she bought him an expensive shirt, a piece of music, something frivolous he would never buy for himself, he would thank her, but look miserable. He seemed to desire nothing. His reaction never failed to make her feel badly. It made her good intentions feel suspect. It made her feel as if she really didn't know him, that she didn't know how to touch him; that he was impenetrable. Once, back then, when she sensed his discomfort, she asked him, "Don't you deserve nice things?" "I have you," he said.

He knew nothing about a scarf. He had never received a scarf from her.

She thought he was kidding. She had started knitting the cashmere scarf for him just before he went away that last time. She had meant to finish it and give it to him before he left for Nicaragua. She remembered the jokey note she meant to enclose: "In case you get cold down there without me."

When she decided she wasn't going to see him again, she knitted I LOVE YOU in tiny, almost invisible letters along one fringe, put the scarf in a manila envelope (she remembered barely needing to lick it because the glue was already wet with her tears), and mailed it to his address in Manhattan. She had sent the post-card the following day.

"I made you a scarf," she said and held the arm of the couch to steady herself, deeply upset, thinking he must have forgotten, or perhaps had lost it when he made one of his many trips. She did not want to believe that he'd never received the envelope. "But you never got it, did you." She was trying to convince herself; it felt as if she were hurting him all over again.

"It wasn't easy for you," she said. She knew he understood: her disappearance and refusal to take his calls twelve years before, her seeming change of heart. "I'm sorry."

He thought about the meaning of "I'm sorry" in Swahili. In Swahili, the speaker was not apologizing, and was not accepting responsibility when she said, I'm sorry. She was simply explaining. In Swahili, sorry meant only: What a shame.

A voice he'd forgotten existed. A voice from far off. A voice of love, or was he mistaken? He would need to hear it from Lily for weeks before he believed it. He understood that he loved her and this suddenly filled him with sadness. He couldn't stand to think what an idiot he'd been that spring (when he lingered in the jungles of central America), and that summer (when he returned, but didn't go to find her). Maybe in his heart he believed he could wait Lily out, whatever reason she needed to escape him would disappear, and she would come back to him.

She had chosen marriage and its single possibility. But he sensed that now perhaps she was again interested in other chances. Or was he mistaken here, too? "You'll know I wasn't finished with you," she'd written twelve years before. He was unsure of just about everything at the moment except the simple fact of Lily next to him.

She lightly touched her index finger to her lips and moved it to his face, easy and flowing, reaching just below his lower eyelid where the eyelash had fallen. Just a touch of pressure from her finger, no more than that, connected him to another time. He blew the lash from her drying fingertip. Here we are where we started, he thought in astonishment. What a remarkable thing, a fuse set one thousand miles north of here and what seemed like a thousand years before, slowly burning, essentially unaltered, ready to ignite.

She remembered part of a dream from the night before. She had awoken terrified. She had been saying to Jonathan in the dream, "If I have you for a day, I'll want you for a week. If I have you for a week, I'll want you for another week." She had thought of him nearly every moment since; her view of him changed from minute to minute. But she could destroy her life, Ben's life. She had a child sleeping at home. And she loved Peter; he had done nothing to deserve this. She could pretend not to understand the risks, pretend to believe there was time to have Jonathan *and* attend to her son, but she was frightened and knew why she was frightened. There must be a way to do this, she supposed.

She looked down at Jonathan's hands because she could not meet his gaze. They had gone out to capture fireflies in the early summer when she hadn't understood what she was feeling, but knew it was the sexiest thing she had ever felt, when she couldn't name it for what it was.

"Dinner now?" she suggested, trying to break the tension. She laughed as she had that first time in New York, and then he burst into laughter too, as he had at lunch the day before.

But this time she hadn't thought out everything in advance.

When she tried to compose herself, no thinking was possible. No plan was possible.

He reached into the box and brought out a gift he had carried for all these years. It was a fez he'd found for her in Bombay, with a red band sewn on with purple silk edging. And when he placed it on her head, she was free, on the run, and unclothed in a room full of Indian wall paintings. She felt her hips open, relax;

she was ready to dance. He loved her to be naked. Her body had never failed to please him. In New York, each weekend was a festival, her skin touched as much as it deserved to be touched.

This is not what she had pictured when she let herself in tonight. Or maybe it was. Maybe it was bound to happen one year or another. Was it possible that there would never be enough time passed that she wouldn't be affected by him? How could she refuse what was unfinished? She thought: I am about to make love with a man who is not my husband. Yet she was not frightened or ashamed in all the ways she imagined she might be if this were any man but Jonathan. Her reserve had toppled. She still wanted Jonathan Parrish. She didn't want to rescue herself or forestall disaster for another minute. It was easy to imagine resisting him only when he wasn't next to her.

The heat of her skin. The heat of her eyes so close to his. His lips, how strange his lips felt. Everything in him was alive and softly shining. Of course, he thought, of course. He allowed his mind to drift and wander. Her first apartment in Hartford, the top floor of a triple-decker, was near an elementary school. He had only visited once. Kids playing tag and yelling. Lined up in rows. High voices coming in through the skylights. A tiny, tiny kitchen with a sloping ceiling where the open refrigerator door banged the stove. Jars of figs, dates, raisins, apricots on a wooden ledge.

He remembered her stepping into the bath the first night home after his surgery, her fear of causing him pain if she mistakenly brushed his wound. He had moved her fingers to his scar so she would know not to be afraid. It had taken years to get used to not seeing Lily. Tonight, it was as if twelve years never happened. Life is supposed to finish up where it started, he thought.

She touched him as though he was the fountain downstairs and she was the little girl running her hands through the water, her fingers like five fins through his hair, across his rough face. Her hand rested on his cheek. Lulled, her vision grew blurry. She felt like a sea creature thrown by a swell of new feeling onto land. Her life of a day ago was gone.

"You could have another with me," he said. "I would love to have a baby with you."

He must have known it would make her cry. Time had not soothed that wound. She wept because she thought she had put this desire away and its reappearance was especially painful surrounded by Jonathan's warmth. She wept because in an instant the image of a little girl was vivid in her mind. She had wanted the second child to be a girl whom she could name Cynthia. She wept because it suddenly seemed possible.

She remembered turning out the light in the bedroom of his New York apartment and standing in the dark. He would listen as she took off her clothes. And it was exciting for her, his listening silence, before she slid in beside him. "Are you ready?" he would ask, with amusement and passion. Before she could answer, he would always interrupt, "*I* am." There were times when he had left her raw, when she'd been too young to say anything in her own defense, when she felt her wants had to be his wants. She had always been struck by the heat of his body, and she remembered nights passing when she did not know if words had been spoken, only that his arms wound around her, held her tightly with continuous changing pressure.

"I understand you are the second half of my life," he said softly. He withdrew her hand from his cheek, held it loosely and stood, gazing gratefully at Lily, by now one of his oldest friends, at her long lovely face. Because she was silent, lost in thought, her wrinkles had vanished and she looked like a young woman. He hoped she would not speak, but would stay motionless for a long while. That she would not move for the next forty-three years.

She was nervous, her palms were moist. "I was scared of you," she said.

The remark startled him as it had when he'd read it in the message she'd left him that morning. He still wasn't sure exactly what she meant. Was it partly an attack: you could have made it easier for me back then? Was it partly a waiving of responsibility? But her tone now included an element of: I'm not scared any longer. I can withstand your force.

He knew when she began to tear up there was something she wasn't saying. And he knew, instinctively, it had to do with her son, not some imagined, future child. You couldn't work in the Third World all your life and not know about mothers and children. Mothers were the only bulwark against chaos in every country he'd seen. It was no different here.

They used to speak of extravagances. What was her source of greatest pleasure, trouble, frustration, fear, yearning, suffering, joy? He knew that the answer to all of these was her son. Her son was the source.

They ran their eyes over each other's face in intimate connection, a gaze of enormous intensity, smiling. Their thoughts were similar and they knew they were. Each knew what the other was looking for because they were looking for the same. He tucked her hair behind her ears and softly kissed her.

"And now what are you most afraid of?" he asked. But he knew the answer.

"I have to make a call home," she said.

Although he believed her, it wasn't true. She had spoken to Ben and her husband a few hours before. She wanted Jonathan to call her bluff. She wanted him to say, "No, don't call. There's no time. I'm ready this minute. Are you?"

"Of course." He became grave, respectful, when he said it, his long bony fingers jammed into his pockets. "Let me walk you to the door."

Who would be ready, after so many years? I am, she thought. Her plane was leaving in twelve hours.

LILY

She was surprised how the evening had ended. So abruptly. She had left and he hadn't stopped her. She'd wanted him to stop her. She had perhaps misjudged some things.

Back in her room, so small after the Presidential Suite, she felt a chill. She couldn't remember if she'd left the window open—to let the New Orleans humidity drift in—or closed, forgetting to turn down the air conditioner as she usually did. The room was unbearably over-cooled. She'd locked the window, it turned out, and when she opened it now, she heard the sounds of brass instruments. Below, the French Quarter was laid bare in its night grid. With no leaf shade, she could see down each congested, neon-blinking street, and a block in, she spotted a group of boys in red band uniforms with gold epaulets: a tuba, a trumpet, a French horn, a drummer. Had she missed the parade? The makeshift band was loud in syncopation and she realized the evening had taken something out of her. She sat on the floor beside the window, her thoughts disordered.

He hadn't asked her to stay; she had been on the verge of settling in without being asked.

She was thirsty, but didn't know if she wanted another beer or black coffee. Near the hot window, her body temperature was confused. Restless, almost frantic, she had the feeling that she was about to break out laughing in a deranged sort of way. At the same time she felt exhausted, dazed. She had the strong urge to straighten the room, and also the desire to pull back the covers and lay across her bed. Life seemed both amazingly complicated and very simple.

She crossed the room and tried to shake off the effects of the visit. Muffled television sounds came through the wall behind her pillows, and although she suddenly felt conspicuously alone in a city a thousand miles from home, the noise comforted her. That she and Jonathan could have lost touch for such a long time seemed possible again. Yet now that she had found him, it seemed impossible to let him go for another twelve years.

She thought of going back up to his room to ask what had happened so she wouldn't have to think about it anymore.

He wasn't ready to make love to her. That was clear: not tonight. He had always been ready for that, but tonight he had looked wistful and contemplative when she left. She didn't like considering the possibility that Jonathan didn't love her. Maybe she had misjudged. At the door, she had kissed him on the mouth, a moment, a little more.

She had offered a reason and broken off the evening, and she wondered what kind of person she was that she was now trying so hard to understand why he hadn't objected. He wasn't ready for marriage, she supposed, its daily repetitions, its obligations and conventions. She wasn't surprised he'd never married. He was fitted primarily to live alone. Wasn't this Jonathan Parrish's great failing?

Maybe the real reason he'd never married was simpler: he was a creep and a jerk. As her father had always suspected. And she, her father's daughter, had taken his side rather than her lover's twelve years before. Maybe Jonathan had been nasty, poisonous, to the women in his life; he'd made their lives impossible as he would have made hers over time. She felt sorry for them for a moment, then sorry for herself. But this assessment seemed wrong: from all she had seen and heard, Jonathan Parrish was as she recalled—adventurous, sincere, generous, hopeful—with the hard edges now smoother.

Not that they had spoken of marriage. Not tonight, not ever.

They had spent fewer than eight hours together and she was thinking of leaving her life in Maine. She felt the encumbrance of decisions made long ago.

She remembered skating on the small pond down the slope behind Jonathan's house. Out the Parrish's kitchen door, through the mud room, outside along the crumbling stone wall, past the dried, ice-encrusted rose bushes following a path of old paving stones set into the brown grass. There was a wrought iron bench under a towering oak tree just beside the pond where you could put on your skates. She had skated on it as a girl, recalling the different alertness of chill air. There were always plenty of people around the frozen surface on a bright January morning. Had Jonathan been there on the day she was thinking of?

There was a strange glow to hotel rooms, even with the television off. A ghostly white from a bathroom night-light, a dense gold shimmer reflecting the wallpaper. An hour before it had seemed as if she and Jonathan were going backward through her life, back together this time.

She had made no pleas; why did it seem like she had? She was tired, her mind flooded with predictable thoughts. She wondered if there was some way he disapproved of her. His not asking her to stay tonight suggested, perhaps, that he simply wasn't ready for scandal. He wasn't ready for a woman whose thinking he didn't know anymore, who had the rounded belly of motherhood, whose lips were too thin, and elbows too pointed, who had white hair mixed with the red now, who would inevitably bore him, who lived a married life with no hazards before he arrived, and had promised a life of continuity to others.

JONATHAN

Despite all his travels, and all he had seen in the wake of war and global misery, despite the vivid reminders that life could suddenly get better if one simply waited, that better days were coming if one was patient, he had never believed this for himself.

He had been unexpectedly nervous and unskillful, disbelieving and clumsy, around Lily. When she'd returned to her room, it felt like a punishment, a deprivation.

When she sat beside him on the couch, he'd thought: when you're in love, you can stay quiet in the world, you don't have to move an inch, you can just stay together in one posture and not do a thing. She had always made the first moves.

He waited an hour and knocked on Lily's door. When she opened, he held out the artichokes on their small white plastic plates, cool now. Forty-eight hours ago they had been two other people, at a distance, out of focus.

Artichokes. The sensuousness of layers peeled away, dipping the sharp-tipped leaves in melted butter, the sliding and pulling and show of teeth, the oils and drips. Artichokes: inconvenient, messy, wondering whether all the trouble was worth it. Reaching the hidden heart, a small victory. He wanted what everyone wanted: everything.

"Let me drive you back to Maine. I'm heading that way, you know. Take an extra day, but I'd get you there. I'd have some more time with you."

PART 6: SUNDAY MORNING

LILY

A m I in the grip of a childish dream? Can the power of memory lift away reality for a time? Have I reassumed an old identity or have I been transformed in preparation of beginning another life? When I said to him, "I'll never let you out of my sight again," was I being rhetorical or was it a promise I intended to keep? Should I not have agreed to meet him at all? If someone you love disappears and you never find out what happened to him, is that any better? Is all of this inevitable or none of it?

To these questions she had no answers as she reread what she had written in her diary after Jonathan had left with his invitation to drive north. Already, she wasn't sure she trusted her memory. Her words on the page were more vivid than memory this morning. She had written: Is it possible that we really didn't make love when it feels on my nipples and in my toes and along my spine as if we did?

Last night she had been scared by how susceptible she was to him, and at times she felt shy, and this mortified her. She remembered putting her hands over her face, half-meaning, half-pretending to cover her shame. But at the same time she wanted to be found out, explored, discovered by Jonathan Parrish.

She was still scared of Jonathan, but in a different way now. It wasn't easy to keep her hands from shaking. She couldn't remember exactly when the shaking started. It was difficult to connect this morning with any she'd had in the past month, the past year, the past twelve years, the repetition of those other mornings superseded by this one. To understand what had happened this weekend was asking too much. She thought of it in the simplest terms: too much emotion stretched over too many hours.

The fear set in at exactly 10:35 PM—she was touching her watch nervously and noticed the time—when she realized that she had always expected from the future only what she knew of the present. But with the present changing, the future was in doubt. One part of her mind jumped through a series of decisions—leave her husband, get a divorce, ask Jonathan to marry her—as a second part of her mind spotted the faulty rapidity of her thoughts. She recalled those days when she played the flute, and it seemed that the faster she played the wrong notes the better, because that way they didn't last long. She was scared she was going to make a mistake.

After eleven years of marriage, when did she kiss anymore like she'd kissed Jonathan last night at her door: wet, wide-open mouths, wordlessly, instantly, fully, wildly? When was the last time she flushed in front of her husband, a magnificent red because of him, for him? She pictured herself at home in the next days. She would have every intention of being cheerful, but she would be tense, edgy, dug into her own dark mood, her gestures forced and false.

Ben.

What was Jonathan Parrish offering with his artichokes? A love affair? A friendship? A new life? She still wasn't sure. What would happen next became vaguer, but more powerful with every passing hour. She couldn't think of a time when Jonathan's manner had changed toward her in the last two days. In many ways he was as he had always been: unhurried in his movements, patient, waiting for her to decide. What was she going to do?

There was nothing to do.

She could leave right away; that was the most sensible solution. Sit at the airport until her plane boarded. Yet she couldn't leave. What had been satisfactory yesterday, a lunch with him in the hotel coffee shop, was strangely inadequate now. Her head was spinning gently. She longed to have dinner with Jonathan again tonight, and breakfast tomorrow, and to run away with him.

To distract herself, she pulled from her suitcase an almost-finished sweater she hadn't touched in years. Cynthia had given her this beautiful ribbon. The yarn was so delicate that the slightest dry skin, nail roughness, or needle irregularity caught on it. Today, she couldn't find the imperfection she remembered, and put the thing away.

Nothing was as it should be. It seemed like an impossible request: drive to Maine with Jonathan. She had woken up with an unambiguous and unblemished joy so intense it awakened a second wave of shame and guilt in her. What would she tell her husband today? Ben was expecting her. She was astonished that she was on the threshold of accepting Jonathan's offer.

She remembered the dream. "If I have you for a day, I'll want you for a week."

She put on black pants and chose for a necklace a simple gold chain. She put her make-up back on, drew her hair up. She needed to walk. Despite the gray sky, she put on sunglasses for their elegance and unapproachability; she didn't want others to see her tear-stained eyes. She rode the elevator down. The atrium seemed strangely large and empty. After the crowds of yesterday, only a few teachers wearing white name tags stood talking, voices low, at eight in the morning.

She had nowhere to go so she set off walking wherever the next street led her. It was Sunday and she passed an elderly couple holding hands, the man in a white linen suit with a red handkerchief tucked into his pocket, observing the formality of the past, his wife gray-haired and stylish with delicate features and beautiful, youthful washed-out blue eyes, wearing a small red hat not unlike the fez she had left on her suitcase. Why couldn't she leave New Orleans as long as Jonathan was here? When would she see him again?

Jonathan loved her. Even if she couldn't love him back, there was this desire to be loved by him again. There was something horrible about the thought of turning away from him again now that he had found her.

Her father's lies, her concessions to Clare's pressure, and her own anger and disappointment in the nightmare days after Cynthia's death caused her to fail him once. Naturally, Jonathan never said that last night, and he wasn't in the least likely to, either. He'd always been gentle. She remembered his gentle hands on her, the whisper of his voice, his lips lingering softly. She had failed him. Maybe she should say it, and it would be out in the open. "I'm sorry," wasn't enough.

But then again he had not responded, "I forgive you," or "It wasn't your fault," or "I got over it," or "It wasn't fair," or "I hated you." He had passed right by these answers.

She generally didn't have much breakfast during the week, but having missed dinner, she was almost painfully hungry. As she searched for a café, she thought of having a meal that would please him: macaroni and cheese, chocolate pudding. Soft foods loved by old people and children and Jonathan. The menu she had made for him the one time he had visited her apartment in Hartford.

She had never liked traveling alone, and that's what it felt like on her search for a quiet place to sit and eat. The rawness of her pain had in no way healed over, and as she walked, she wondered what comfort the past really offered and what her true feelings had been when her love affair with Jonathan ended.

She found a family-owned neighborhood place with a sandwich board outside offering a crawfish special and, once inside, took a table in a corner. After she ordered, she reached into her bag for her book of *Magnificent Trees* while her waiter finished something he'd been saying that she didn't quite catch.

Suddenly, she remembered the second part of her dream from the night before. She remembered why she had awoken frightened. She had been saying to Jonathan in the dream, "If I have you for a day, I'll want you for a week. If I have you for a week, I'll want you for another week." Then she had noticed Ben, sitting on the ground a few yards away, looking up at her and crying.

A red Mustang passed outside the restaurant and she thought of that year in her life with Jonathan as driving in a convertible—the top down, wind in her eyes, the illusion of constant perfect speed. For some reason she remembered the word the shopkeeper in the market around the corner from Jonathan's apartment always called her: radiant.

She felt like a lunatic ordering a Hurricane, the town's famous cocktail, this early in the day, but she was already washed-out, powerless. She'd already lost her equilibrium; why not?

Nothing could equal the recollection of being young together. She was at first shocked that this feeling was so easily available to her, that Jonathan could touch her and she could realize she had never forgotten his fingers searching her skin. It seemed so right then and it seemed so right now.

Peter was probably lying on the couch now, watching football, trying to interest Ben in the sport. Ben was an expression of their marriage, their love. She wasn't the kind to humiliate her husband. She loved her husband in a way that included both irritation and compassion. He couldn't help the way he was; he couldn't help that he wasn't Jonathan Parrish.

She must live her normal life, with its dailiness of compromise and acceptance, its waxing and waning lightness, making the best of things.

No. She understood there were obstacles, but what better way to express her love than to drive north with him? Jonathan Parrish had an immeasurable faith in love and she was ready to match his. She was in peril of gambling away this second chance and she did not expect Jonathan to come to her again. She was ready to join him. She tried hard to talk herself out of this decision, but failed. At least everything would be clear. The rules that she had taken for twelve years as her laws of caution regarding Jonathan Parrish were suspended. She couldn't turn her back on him and flee. It had nothing to do with reason. It was the same illogic that brought them together before. Would she be happier today if she had gone with him then? she wondered. Now she was ready to take the side of daring and madness. Since she had always been a little scared of him, she wanted to prove this fear was ridiculous. Last night, when Jonathan said, "You are the second half of my life," she did not know how or what she should feel.

Once again she had the strange feeling that what was happening was not real, could not be real: she was thinking of starting a scarf. Contrary to what she supposed she ought to feel, she was genuinely happy. If this weekend secret were kept, she would have no regrets. But when she said this to herself, she thought: who am I trying to convince? In a few months, she hoped she would think: New Orleans was a long time ago. However superficially strange or shocking, this weekend with Jonathan had an unsurprising, familiar quality that invited her to say, Yes of course, I was expecting that.

She indulged herself. She let herself believe that she belonged with Jonathan, and when she did, a feeling of relief passed over her, of old confusions and obligations wiped away. After breakfast, she would walk back to the hotel and tell him.

She thought about where to put the fez in her classroom.

JONATHAN

When he had climbed into his truck in Vermont two days before, he was aware, as he often was when he shut the door and threw his bag over his shoulder into the storage space behind the front seat, of his inner restlessness. It had always been there, its source never identified. Usually, this restlessness was dissipated by a destination. But with New Orleans and Lily, it had instead acquired a new intensity.

How long had it taken between the moment he met her again and the moment he recognized her for the woman he loved? Would he be as moved and enchanted day after day with her as he was today or was this urgency, this ravishment, due to her vanishing once before?

He realized that he was merely trying to disillusion himself. Like so many times these past two days, images or remembered moments crossed his mind and he couldn't shake them off. The way she slept, deeply, like an animal, which he envied. The rhythm of her hips when she rode a bicycle uphill. The way she put her hand in the pocket of his coat when they walked like lovers, shoulders touching. She was exactly the right size for him when they stood face to face. Lily had set him thinking. He knew no ambivalence regarding Lily. His life felt as if it existed only for her.

He blamed himself, he blamed her, but he had never delivered himself to her to ask why it had ended between them because, he believed, it would have made no sense to him. He knew all he needed to know at thirty. When it ended, it was hard not to think that losing Lily was the end of everything that mattered. Everyone believed love affairs were going to last, didn't they? He had been helpless to correct his lost faith in love until he saw her at the table over yesterday's lunch. He had not lived in the past, the year of their love affair, expecting that it would miraculously return.

The heat, which he had always enjoyed, abruptly felt like too much of a good thing. The Presidential Suite was now a room they had shared and was still haunted by her recent presence. He had never minded being laughed at by Lily, and now he chuckled at himself. Of course, she hadn't answered his offer to drive her back to Maine. What could she say? It was like asking her to come to Nicaragua with him when she was twenty-three. Impossible. She wasn't ready. He was gripped by an enormous compassion for her.

Where was she when he wanted to tell her everything he'd been thinking overnight? Having breakfast with a colleague, he assumed. He listened to the radio as he cleaned up the dishes. The newscaster's voice was full of all that had gone wrong in the world that day. The man had a tone of resignation, of frail recollection, as if everything he was reporting had happened without anyone's approval.

Remembering everything, he felt the present dominated by the past and its unconfirmed assumptions. Until this morning, he tried to guess what was in her mind, but now he had to keep the imagined workings of her brain at bay as he considered what was best.

Beneath the bravado that might allow her to accept his offer, she was a sensitive woman. A trip north, following her heart, would cause her a lot of pain she couldn't foresee. She would repeat the arguments over and over in her head until she made peace with what she would say to her husband. But how would she ever break the news to her son? He would not understand; he would have only the tiniest sense of what was happening. What would he know except that he had lost his mother, or some part of her?

Jonathan knew he had no business taking Lily away from her son, even for a few days. He felt the strange sensation of fatigue that came from having awakened something inside him that should have remained asleep. He didn't want Lily to choose, to have to make a choice, because she would feel she had no choice this time around. She wasn't in any right sort of state to make a decision now.

He allowed himself to close his eyes. He saw the figure of himself in his Vermont house, standing alone. He was aware of sadness, aware his mind could never again empty itself of Lily Mayeux.

He had been cheated of her before, but she was no longer his; she belonged to Ben. And a child had no interest in interrogating the past. Women were mothers first. Jonathan knew this intuition was no trick of his tired mind. He felt the asymmetry of their lives. His decision was weighted with fear, but tinged with impatience and self-contempt. He lighted the cigarette he'd been ready to start on since he'd woken up. Then he began to cry.

He started to pack up the items that belonged in his shoe box, collecting them from the tables and chairs and couches of the living room. She had examined each one and placed it on a different surface so that she could stand back and study the full panorama of his love. The green silk purse. The hand-painted ivory earrings. The tiny birdcage and the thick bronze bracelet. She had taken with her only the red fez. He would leave before lunch.

Why give up what made him feel subtle and happy and alive? The strength to leave Lily came from what had happened between them these past two days. The indestructible yearning for things that weren't and never could be. He imagined the long drive home, the windows of the truck rolled open—he liked the clean motion of windows controlled by the turning of handles— holding the steering wheel, familiar and not familiar, caressing it as if he could administer it pleasure. It took all his effort to restrain himself from phoning her room.

He sat down to write the note he would leave her. He wanted to warn her about the injury he was about to inflict, but phrased it like a telegram: "Unexpected obligation. Had to leave town early. You'll know that I wasn't finished." His profession had always allowed him to be vague about destinations and reasons. Was there another way to do this?

He did not see that he could act otherwise. Knowing her, he was sure she would understand after the initial hurt, that this wasn't about revenge or retribution, but the unbearable present and the privileged status of the past. She would know that this was the only thing he could do for her, for them both, today. He knew the power of the weekend had been about Lily beginning to think of him again. She now knew something about his life, and he would be in her mind from now on, alive. And he would be happy to know she was thinking of him. It was not regret that assailed him as he packed his black bag, but something less sure, less defined, and he wondered how many years would have to pass before he would see her the next time.

PART 7: ARRIVAL

I was born a loved and wanted child two years after this weekend in New Orleans when my mother was thirty-eight and my father was forty-six and my half brother Ben was seven. I too knit, but not as well as my mother Lily; I too travel to places of war and empty stomachs and disease, but not as often as my father Jonathan. Each day I write in a journal bound in thick boards like the red and black volumes my parents gave me, when I turned twenty-one, concerning their lives and my beginning. Their words about themselves are like storytelling to me, almost invented.

Sometimes we fall in love before we know it's happening. Sometimes we forget the past, but only because we want to. Sometimes, we refuse one future and demand another.